A KILLING WAY

A KILLING WAY

A Nate Ross Novel

J.R. Sanders

First published by Level Best Books/Historia 2024

Copyright © 2024 by J.R. Sanders

All rights reserved. No part of this publication may be reproduced, stored or transmitted in any form or by any means, electronic, mechanical, photocopying, recording, scanning, or otherwise without written permission from the publisher. It is illegal to copy this book, post it to a website, or distribute it by any other means without permission.

This novel is entirely a work of fiction. The names, characters and incidents portrayed in it are the work of the author's imagination. Any resemblance to actual persons, living or dead, events or localities is entirely coincidental.

J.R. Sanders asserts the moral right to be identified as the author of this work.

First edition

ISBN: 978-1-68512-704-6

Cover art by Level Best Designs

This book was professionally typeset on Reedsy.
Find out more at reedsy.com

To the sisters— Judi, Pat, and Jeanette— for always being there, always supportive. If I've never said it, I'm saying it here. Thanks.

Praise for the Nate Ross Novels

"Nate Ross, a PI with a rhythm and poetry all his own, navigating the City of Angels with clipped wings."—Craig Johnson, author of the Walt Longmire series

"Ace Atkins fans should give this series a look."—*Publishers Weekly*

Chapter One

Hollywood's always been a place where art imitates life and, more often than not, the other way around. The shooting of Ty Jones by Leo Rust was a primo example of the latter. It took place not in Hollywood proper but in Griffith Park, a rustic oasis in the middle of L.A.'s metropolitan sprawl, in the early fall of 1939. But it could easily have happened in Dodge City or Deadwood in the wild old days. And more accurately, I guess, it was life imitating art imitating life. Only in L.A.

I'd read about it in all the papers—you couldn't live in this city and avoid it. And I'd heard varying and conflicting accounts from the cowpokes who played the part of bandits and ranch hands in Tinseltown's B-films by day and haunted the Buscadero, my pal Dusty's bar, by night. Every one of them claimed to be an eyewitness, although if even a fraction of them had really been there, the cops would still be taking statements.

When you sorted out the known facts from the exaggerations, hooptedoodle, and outright lies, what was left over went something like this: On a clear, sunny, Indian summer morning in early October, the cowboys were assembled per usual at the Columbia Drugstore on Sunset at Gower. *Gower Gulch*, the film folk called it. The drug store's pay phone was their pipeline to Central Casting, where they each hoped to line up work for the day, or several days if they were lucky, on one of the horse operas Poverty Row—the small-budget studios—churned out. Or better yet, on a film for one of the bigger houses, which meant a much longer shoot.

Rust was sitting at the store's lunch counter working on his steak and eggs when Jones walked in. The boys all took immediate interest since it was common knowledge, or so they all claimed later, that there was bad blood between the two men. The story was that they'd started on friendly terms; they'd known each other since the Midwest migration had brought Jones to town a year or so earlier. But the friendship had soured of late owing, cowboy gossip held, to Jones's undue attention to Rust's wife, Hazel. Witnesses to their meeting that day were unanimous in agreement that from the get-go, Rust clearly had (as one witness put it) "a burr under his saddle." He evil-eyed Jones starting the moment he entered. Jones, meanwhile, said cheery hellos to several of the cowboys, gradually making his way to where Rust sat fuming in his coffee.

Only then, they said, did Jones even appear to notice that Rust was present. He offered Rust a similar salutation, and Rust responded with a grunt and a muttered curse. The exact wording was a matter of some dispute, but in any case, was unprintable in the newspaper reports.

Jones showed no sign of having taken offense, but grinned and asked, "Why, what's eating at you today, Leo?"

Rust, the cowboys said, swiveled his stool to face Jones dead on and stared at him for a good five seconds before he spoke. When he did, it was in a flat, measured tone. Everyone present agreed on those words: "Don't fool with me, son. I'm in a killing way today."

Jones seemed to take no more note of the veiled threat than he had the epithet. After a moment's pause, he said, "All right, then," winked at Rust and sauntered away. Rust's eyes tracked him until he faded into the crowd on the sidewalk outside.

The lunch counter confrontation made things understandably tense when both men turned up at Bronson Canyon, in Griffith Park, a couple of hours later. Each had been picked to fill out the cast of a western for one of the low-budget studios. Bit parts, both of them, the sort of non-speaking background roles that were the Hollywood cowpoke's bread and butter. Jones was assigned to portray one of the hapless hired hands defending the ranch from a bandit gang. Rust, owing to his scruffy and surly looks, was one of the bandits. In the scene they were filming, the gang was to come thundering in on horseback, while the ranch hands took cover in and around a rickety line

CHAPTER ONE

shack and among the surrounding rocks. General gunfire and mayhem were then to ensue. On a picture with a bigger budget, the scene would have been carefully choreographed, but in a cheap oater like this one, it was mostly improvised, with the boys given next to nothing in the way of direction.

All was going according to Hoyle when Rust, in his role of desperado, potted a rifle shot in Jones's direction, and Jones gave out with a realistic cry of pain and an unscripted but dramatic fall. Bruce Clarkson, the annoyed director, yelled "Cut!" and stormed over to bawl out the day player for hamming it up. His irritation only grew when Jones kept his face planted in the dirt as the director commenced his tirade. Clarkson assumed he was being made the victim of cowboy hijinx until he observed that the dust under Jones's chest was turning to mud. With the help of one of the other extras, he rolled the cowboy over to discover that he was stone dead, with a bullet hole square in the middle of his chest.

Pandemonium broke out, and by the time it fully dawned on the director what had happened and what needed to be done, Rust was nowhere to be found. He'd thrown down the rifle and, in the words of one cowboy, "lit a shuck."

He wasn't on the lam for long. The L.A. coppers picked him up three hours later at a streetcar stop two blocks from his apartment. He stood the pinch without a fuss.

The shooting caused an immediate split in the cowboy crowd, with one side claiming Rust was a dirty, dry-gulching skunk (their words) and the other calling Jones a miserable, perfidious, snaky son of a bitch, who, if the world was fair and just probably ought to have been shot in the cradle. Discussions of the matter tended to get pretty heated, even between Dusty and his business partner, Pooter, who fell on opposite sides.

It didn't help matters when the District Attorney's office declined to file criminal charges against Rust, despite sworn statements from over a dozen cowboys who had witnessed the confrontation between Rust and Jones and overheard Rust declaring himself to be "in a killing way." The decision, D.A. Buron Fitts told the press, was based primarily on the fact that the empty cartridge casing left in the Winchester carbine Rust had fired the fatal shot from, had unidentified fingerprints on it. Not Rust's and not, according to the detectives that investigated, belonging to anyone working on the set that day.

Rust claimed that he had only run after shooting Jones out of panic, not guilt. His story was that he'd been as shocked as anyone when he realized he'd fired a live round at Jones. He said he'd been given the rifle, presumably loaded with blanks, by the film's prop master, Ed Stovall, about half an hour prior to the shooting. He claimed he'd left it propped against a wall when he used the park's men's room for a "quick piss," no more than two or three minutes, and it had otherwise been in his possession the entire time.

This account, if it was true, seemed at first to put the finger on the prop man. The cops were not able to talk to Stovall, because he had followed Rust's lead and faded after the shooting. The locked ammo chest he left behind was not found to contain any other live ammunition, only various calibers of blank loads.

While the D.A.'s office passed on charging Rust, the L.A. police were keeping their investigation open. They were unsure, in Stovall's absence, whether they were dealing with a deadly accident or something nastier. In the meantime, D.A. Fitts maintained his stand that there wasn't sufficient evidence—yet, anyway—to charge Rust with manslaughter, let alone murder. Either, he no doubt figured would have been a crap shoot, and nobody's ever made a nickel betting on what an L.A. jury would do.

Three days after the D.A.'s decision was on page one of all the local rags, I dropped into the Buscadero. With all the heated talk over the shooting, Dusty and Pooter had made the bar a neutral corner by declaring all discussions of the shooting, or of its principal players, off limits. They'd likewise raised the white flag between the two of them. The moratorium hadn't eliminated problems altogether. There was still a fair amount of tension, plenty of angry looks and muttered remarks, and even the occasional scuffle. But at least it kept most of the hostility under the surface. I did my best to keep my opinions about it to myself, hoping to help keep the peace. I figured all along it was a forlorn hope. The thing was a keg of dynamite waiting to blow, and all I could do was try to be standing clear of the danger zone when it did.

CHAPTER ONE

***

I'd only come in to pick up my dog. I'd left him with Dusty and Pooter while I was at work, to keep him from tearing up my backyard in his never-ending, self-appointed mission to depopulate Los Angeles of gophers. The bar, as usual, was nice and cool inside. It was a sweet relief to step out of the heat after baking in my car in Pacoima for half the day watching the house of a guy who was supposed to be selling lumber out of his garage—stuff he'd boosted from a housing tract under construction in the Valley. I get all the glamour jobs.

Pooter hailed me as I took a seat at the bar with his customary "Pooter there, pard!"—a joke he never tired of—accompanied by a bone-crunching handshake. He wasn't a big man, but the guy had forearms like Popeye and a grip like a bear trap. Without asking, he slid a cold mug of beer in front of me, and I wrapped my aching fingers around it. Dusty was nowhere in sight, so Pooter bellowed, "Dusty! Company!"

Dusty came out of the back room lugging a carton of bottles which he deposited on the far end of the bar. "Howdy, Nate. How goes the Great Lumber Heist of 1939?"

"It goes to pay the rent, if I'm lucky."

Dusty strode down the bar to offer a less painful handshake, with Monte following close at his heels. The big dog had perked up when he spotted me, and without invitation, he clambered up and perched his furry butt on the stool next to me. He rested his front paws on the bar, gave me a wide canine smile, and unrolled his long tongue in a yawn.

"Hey there, you ornery cuss." Pooter extended a hand, and Monte plopped a big red paw into it. "You thirsty?" Pooter ruffled the dog's ears and brought a bowl of water out from under the bar. He set it down, and Monte lapped at it happily, slopping about half of it onto the bar top.

"Sorry about that." I reached over the bar for a towel and started sopping up the mess.

Pooter grinned and waved a hand in dismissal. "Hell, he ain't half as sloppy as most of our customers."

Dusty took a seat on the other side of Monte. He ran a hand across the big dog's back. "Say, Nate. If you can tear yourself away from all that excitement in Pacoima, I might could put you on to somethin' more in your line."

"What would that be?"

"Do you know Bill Hart?"

I thought a moment "You talking about the Pasadena copper? No, wait, his name's Hartman." I searched my brain a little longer. "I give up—who's Bill Hart?"

For an answer, he pointed to the wall behind the bar. Along with a big, oval mirror and a framed color lithograph of a Western scene showing a gaggle of cowboys firing pistols into the air as they tried to ride their horses into a hotel, there were framed photos of various movie cowboys. The one Dusty pointed out was of a horse-faced fellow pointing two six-guns at the camera and looking out from under his wide hat brim, with a steely expression. Scrawled slantwise next to the grim face, I read, "Sincerely yours, William S. Hart."

It took the tumblers a second to click. I wasn't much of a movie fan anymore, but as a kid, I'd gone to my share of films with my old man. His taste ran to Westerns, and now that I looked at the photo on the wall, it came back to me. William S. Hart had been one of my father's favorites. His silent films were gritty and realistic, and he generally played some sort of square John character—the kind of straight-talking, upright soul who'd never spit in front of a lady or shoot a guy in the back. He'd been no young buck back then, and I couldn't remember hearing of a movie he'd made since I was in high school. If anybody had asked me, I'd have figured the guy was long dead.

"Okay." I looked back at Dusty. "I remember him. What about him?"

"He wants to hire you."

"Hire me. To do what?"

"Well, I'd rather you get that from the horse's mouth, so to speak." He explained that he'd bumped into Hart at one of the movie ranches up in Newhall, thirty miles or so north of the city—Hart apparently lived on a ranch of his own nearby—and the actor had brought up a problem he was having. Knowing Dusty had been a lawman in his salad days, Hart inquired

CHAPTER ONE

whether he might know someone who could help, and Dusty had suggested me. He wouldn't tell me more than that, and I knew it was a waste of time and breath to ask. We made arrangements to drive out to Hart's place together the next morning so I could hear the story from the man himself.

With that out of the way for now, I couldn't help breaching the house rules and asking. "Are things simmering down any on the Rust business?"

Dusty and Pooter exchanged a look before Dusty said a word. Pooter turned his back and started futzing with bottles. Even Monte seemed to get that it was a dicey subject. He looked at each of the old cowboys with his ears up, then gave me what I read as an accusing look, as if to say, "Why the hell would you bring that up?"

"There's still some hard feelings on both sides," Dusty said at last. "We ain't had to break up any fights lately, but you can sort of smell it in the air when the boys are here."

Pooter spoke over his shoulder. "It don't help that that son—" his eyes flicked toward Dusty in the mirror. "That *Rust's* showed back up on a couple of sets."

"Man's got to eat," Dusty muttered.

Pooter opened his mouth to chip back at Dusty but thought better of it.

Dusty looked at me. "I don't suppose you'd consider just takin' a look…"

"Not a chance. Stick my head in that hornet's nest? The cops looked at it and the D.A.'s declined to file it. And I've got enough enemies downtown already."

"I guess you're right," Dusty said. "But I ain't none too sure that things will ever be like they were. These boys have long memories."

I looked around at the empty tables. "Well, I just hope it doesn't hurt your business too much."

"Aw, I'm not worried about that. It's Hollywood—where the hell else are them damn rowdies gonna drink?"

"I guess that's true." I drained the last of my beer and stood up. "Speaking of rowdies," I slapped my leg, and Monte climbed off his stool. "We'd better get you home and fed. Thanks for watching him, boys."

Pooter turned around and gave us a grin and a wave. If he was sore at me for bringing up the shooting, it didn't show. "So long, fellas," he said.

I gave Dusty a two-finger salute. "Pick you up at eight?" He nodded, and Monte and I headed out.

Chapter Two

I left Monte at the office the next morning. Benjy, my pal who worked in his uncle's diner downstairs, promised to keep an eye on him. Dusty was waiting at the curb when I reached the club. I wasn't sure if he and Pooter were on the outs or he was just eager to go, and I didn't ask. If he was anxious, he didn't show it.

"How's the new car workin' out?" Dusty asked as I pulled out into traffic.

"So far, so good." A couple months back, I'd traded my old coupe in for a secondhand Ford sedan. I was still getting used to the flathead eight after having only four cylinders, but the extra space came in handy, especially once I started hauling around an eighty-pound dog. Plus, the new crate didn't have any bullet holes in it. After giving me driving directions to Hart's, Dusty tipped his hat over his eyes and settled back for his customary nap.

Less than an hour later, with his normal uncanny sense, Dusty snapped awake and sat up just in time to direct me off the highway and west down a side road. We drove for a couple of miles until we came upon the entrance to Hart's Horseshoe Ranch. We followed a winding track up the hillside and one of the first things to come in sight was a tall sort of tower. It had the look of adobe, but otherwise could have been something out of Robin Hood. It was round, maybe twenty feet tall, with a heavy wood door at its base, and there were battlements around the top like a medieval fortress. Painted on the side, I read "La Loma de los Vientos."

"Does this guy live in a castle?' I asked Dusty.

He just grinned. "You'll see."

Beyond the tower, the twisting path leveled off, and we found ourselves looking across a broad, green expanse with a large, handsome, Spanish Colonial house sitting to one side. It wasn't a castle, exactly, but it somehow had the feel of one. I pulled up and stopped near the big house's entrance, and before we'd gotten out of the car, the heavy wood front door swung open, and a man stepped out. If he hadn't been dressed in full cowboy duds, including a low-crowned hat with a wide, flat brim, I doubt I'd have known him from either the bar photo or my own memories. William S. Hart, terror to outlaws and evildoers in all those horse operas I'd seen as a kid.

Minus the getup he was just a slight, sad faced, somewhat sickly-looking guy in what I guessed to be his mid-seventies. He approached us with a stiff, shuffling, old man's gait that wasn't helped any by his high-heeled boots. Still, there was a kind of dignity—faded, but not forgotten—in the erect way he carried himself. He gave us a thin smile and stretched out a bony hand when Dusty stepped around the car to meet him.

"Good morning, old compadre." From the characters he'd played in the silent pictures, I'd imagined him speaking with a cowboy drawl, in a low voice, roughed up around the edges from bawling at stray dogies and shouting outlaws out of their hidey holes. His was a good octave higher with a precise, stagey sort of delivery and a slight blurring of his s's.

"Howdy, pard." Dusty gave him a quick handshake and waved his other hand toward me. "This here's Nate Ross. Nate, meet Bill Hart."

"Mr. Ross, of course." Hart's handshake was firmer than he looked capable of. "Dusty tells me you are just the fellow to handle my thorny little problem."

"Well, we'll see," I said. "And call me Nate."

Hart made a sweeping motion towards the house. "Well, welcome to La Loma de Los Vientos." I guess he read on my face that my Spanish was a little shaky. "The Hill of the Winds." He grinned. "Come up here in the evening sometime, and you'll understand the name." He turned towards the house. "Shall we go inside?"

When he opened the door, he was nearly bowled over by a huge black and white dog—a Great Dane so tall Hart could almost have ridden her in one of his movies. The dog frisked past him and ran up to Dusty and me. Dusty crouched and took the dog's big head in both hands and gave her cheeks a

CHAPTER TWO

rub."

Hart looked apologetic. "I'm sorry, gents. She's quite a social creature, and we don't get as many visitors as we used to." He addressed himself to the dog with a laugh. "Gal! Run off and play now, you scamp. Go on!" The dog bounded off across the broad lawn with a happy bark, and a cluster of crows who'd been picking at the grass made irritated squawks as she chased them off.

Hart led us through the doorway into a turreted entryway. Its ceiling was high and had heavy beams radiating out like spokes in a wagon wheel and colorful Indian designs painted around the wheel's circumference. The inside of the house looked as much like a museum as a home. Every place I looked, there were Western bronzes, paintings, framed sketches, and photographs. Brightly colored Navajo rugs and blankets decorated floors, walls, and railings.

Hart led us up a spiral staircase to the upper floor and down an open hallway into a large room filled with rustic furniture. The morning light spilled in through large, red-draped windows on three sides. Big rugs woven with Indian patterns, along with a large bear skin, covered most of the floor, and overhead were dark, heavy, square-hewn beams decorated with more Indian designs. Paintings and photos hung on every wall, with the exception of one spot where a big rectangle of wallpaper had a slightly darker tone. Something had hung there that was not there now.

Hart waved us onto a sofa more comfortable than it looked, and he sat in a big chair between the tiled fireplace and a small side table made of dark wood. He saw me noticing the bare wall space.

"That's the very thing that I'd like to discuss with you, Nate. I've played quite a range of parts over the years. Both good men and bad, although I always tried to show a glimmer of good in even bandits and gunslingers. But now it seems this old desperado has himself fallen prey to black-hearted villains."

"In other words, somebody's knocked you over?"

"Knocked me—?" His puzzled frown shifted to a delighted smile. "Of course. A man in your line would naturally employ the argot of the underworld." He leaned forward. "In King's English, I've been robbed."

I studied the blank wall. "A painting?"

He stood and stepped over to the empty spot on the wall. He turned and faced us, struck a pose, and spoke as if he were addressing a crowded theater. "Not a mere painting, a masterwork. And one with great sentimental as well as pecuniary value. A Russell. The *last* Russell, in fact."

"Russell?"

His dramatic manner dissolved. "*Charlie* Russell, of course." He looked at Dusty. I looked at Dusty. Dusty just shook his head. A slow smile was spreading underneath his big moustache.

"Sorry, Mr. Hart," I said. "I'm afraid I'm not much of an art expert."

"Bill, if you please." He gave me a pitying look and then took his seat again. He spoke to me in a tone that showed sympathy for my ignorance. "Charles Marion Russell was one of the finest artists ever to chronicle our great vanishing frontier. His paintings, drawings, and sculptures have brought the West to life in a way none other have ever captured, or ever will. Not only was he a rare talent, a poet with a paintbrush, but he was an old and dear personal friend."

He choked up at this last statement and took a minute to compose himself. When he had, he explained that he and Russell went back as far as Hart's early days as a stage actor in New York. Over the years, he said, they had "ridden the same trails" and become bosom pals. The painting in question was a portrait of Hart himself that Russell had gifted the old ham with not long before he died a dozen or so years back. It was the last painting he'd ever done.

"Charlie had painted me once before, of course, many years ago," Hart said. "When I was a far younger man and still sat tall in the saddle. But in this portrait," He gestured at the empty spot. "In this one, he captured a more seasoned man, battered a bit by the years and by experience, perhaps, but still sturdy and able. He captured the nobility that I always tried to project in the roles I played. He painted—if not the man I was—at least the man I strove to be." His eyes took on a faraway look, like he was gazing down the long, dusty trail behind him.

CHAPTER TWO

"This painting," I said, trying to snap him back into the present, "You say it's pretty valuable?" Before he could answer, I added, "I mean in a dollars-and-cents kind of way?"

"Naturally." His eyes came back into sharp focus. "Charlie's work hangs in galleries and museums across the country, perhaps across the globe. It's highly sought after by collectors." He waved a hand around the room. "I have a number of his pieces here, and over the years, I've been pestered no end to sell one or another, but I wouldn't part with any of them. But this one…" He started tearing up again. "This one I value more than the lot. More than anything—everything—in this old home of mine. I must have it back."

"All right," I said. "Just so I'm clear, you want to hire me to find out who stole it?"

"Not at all." His gaze sharpened, and a bit of the steely-eyed cowboy returned. "I know very well who stole it. I simply want you to help me get it back."

"I don't follow. If you know who took it, why not go to the police?"

"Two excellent reasons. For one, if I did that, the matter would soon become public. Foolish pride on my part, I suppose, but the image I've crafted over the years is not of a man who could be bested by a petty burglar."

Hollywood. I should have figured ego came into it.

"And the other reason?"

"The man who stole it is dead."

I shot a look at Dusty. He gave me a lopsided grin and spread his hands. "Ty Jones."

I sighed. Leave it to Dusty—he'd found a way to drag me into the fray after all. I turned back to Hart.

"First of all, why are you so certain it was Jones?"

Hart explained that two weeks earlier, he'd allowed a crew from P.R.C. Pictures to shoot some exterior scenes on the ranch property. He'd hung around the set and watched for several hours then had left to have dinner with friends in the city while the crew stayed behind to shoot some dusk scenes. When he'd returned a little before midnight, he'd come into this room to have a nightcap before retiring and had noticed that the painting was gone. He'd immediately checked on his invalid sister, who lived with him and occupied a bedroom upstairs, and had found her safely asleep. Going over the rest of the house, he'd found a downstairs kitchen window that had been jimmied.

"Anything else missing?"

"No, but one thing was left behind." He went over to a secretary desk against one wall, opened a drawer, and removed something. "In the corner below the window, I found this." He handed me what looked like a big silver button—domed, about the size of a half dollar, with a metal loop soldered to the back. It had a scalloped design engraved around the rim, and each scallop was set with a tiny dot of turquoise stone. An engraved eagle spread its wings across the center.

"What is it?" I asked.

"A concho. One of the cowboy extras who was out here that day was wearing a very fine old pair of chaps with identical conchos down the legs." He motioned around the room in explanation. "You may have noticed I'm an avid collector of such items. I didn't know the man by name, though I had seen him before. I hosted a barbecue here for the Western film crews on the Fourth of July, and I recall seeing him in attendance. I remember because I admired those chaps."

He picked up a newspaper from the table. I could see it had a front-page story about the shooting. "And then, when I read about the incident at Griffith Park and saw his photograph, I recognized him instantly."

"Ty Jones."

"I gave tours of the house that day—no doubt that's how he became aware of the painting." He pointed to the concho. "I suppose he must have caught it on the window frame when he climbed through."

"You tell anyone, make any attempts to contact this guy?"

"I told no one save Mamie, and she'd been asleep and heard nothing. I only told Dusty here a couple of days ago because I have been at my wit's end. And I didn't need to contact Jones—he contacted me." He reached into the drawer again and took out a folded sheet of paper, passing it over to me. I unfolded it and read in carefully printed block letters:

CHAPTER TWO

Wild Bill,

If you want your picture back, bring 5,000 dollars cash to the Oak of the Golden Dream at midnight on the 15th. Put it in a plain brown envelope and leave it in the hollow at the base of the tree. Come alone, leave the money, and go. I'll be watching. No cops, no marked bills, and no funny business, or I burn the painting and send you the ashes."

"I received that in the mail two days after the painting went missing."

The note wasn't signed, and there was no return address on the envelope Hart handed me. There wouldn't be. A Hollywood postmark—not much help.

I looked at Hart. "Oak of the Golden Dream?"

"It's a big live oak that sits along the creek bed up Placerita Canyon a few miles from here," Hart said. "Rumored to be the exact spot where one of the Spanish dons found gold several years before the big rush up Sacramento way."

"Did you follow the directions, make the drop?"

"I did. I waited at home afterward but heard nothing. So the very next day, I rode back up to the spot, and there was my envelope with the money untouched." He held up the newspaper. "Now, of course, I understand why."

"Okay, so now Jones is dead, you still have your five grand and no clue what's become of your painting. Right so far?" Hart nodded solemnly.

"I guess I can try and locate it for you. I'm assuming that's what you want from me?"

"It is indeed."

"I can't promise you much. There's no telling what this guy Jones did with it. For all we know, he's already sold it to some third party." Hart paled at the suggestion. "You said yourself Russell's stuff is hot with collectors. I'd imagine his very last painting would be even more—"

"Please just do what you can, Nate." He went back to the secretary, took a thick brown envelope from the drawer, and handed it over. Inside was a crisp stack of fifties and hundreds.

"This is the ransom cash?"

"It was. It's yours now if you'll help me." He sat again. "Please."

I slid out a single C-note and pocketed it. "This'll get us started. We can talk fees once I see what we're dealing with." I held out the envelope. He looked uncertain, so I tossed it on the table beside him.

"Okay if I hang onto the concho?" He nodded, and I pocketed the thing.

He looked at the envelope on the table. "The money doesn't matter to me, Nate. If I can get my painting back..." He threatened to go weepy again, so I stood up to signal that this part of our meeting was over. Dusty stood with me and Hart, taking the cue, wiped his eyes on a shirt cuff and got to his feet.

At my request, we went to the sister's room so I could ask her directly about the night of the theft. Mary Ellen—Mamie, as Hart called her—was a plump, gray-haired old gal who looked to be a few years his junior. Though she was bedridden and had been for some time, according to her brother, she was plenty sharp. Still, she wasn't able to be much help. She said she had read for, by her estimate, about two hours after Bill left for dinner that night and had then slept straight through until morning. That put the burglary anywhere between 7:30 and a quarter to twelve when he came back.

Before Dusty and I left, Bill insisted on giving us a tour of the house and grounds. He pointed out with pride photos of himself with Wyatt Earp, Bat Masterson, Will Rogers, and the portrait painter himself, Charlie Russell. He showed us a few other smaller pieces Russell had done—mostly pen and ink sketches—plus a small bronze sculpture of Will Rogers on horseback, as well as a portrait of Hart himself, also on horseback. It was the earlier one he'd mentioned, and it showed the younger Hart I remembered from all those films. Once we'd gone through the house, top to bottom, Hart insisted on taking us down the hill for a guided walk through the graveyard he'd set aside for his many dogs. He told heartfelt stories about several of them as we passed among the headstones and markers with the dogs' names. The most recent was Prince Hamlet, Hart's other Great Dane. He'd died just the year before, Hart said, and less than two weeks later, he'd also lost his favorite horse, Fritz. The grand finale was a stop at a tall river rock monument that marked Fritz's grave. The monument held a huge bronze plaque with an image of Fritz's head in relief on it. It read:

CHAPTER TWO

BILL HART'S
PINTO PONY
"FRITZ"
AGED 31 YEARS
A LOYAL COMRADE

I'd had no idea horses lived so long. I'd also had no idea someone could be so sentimental about one that he'd build a finer memorial for him than the average person could ever expect to end up under. It told me a lot about Bill Hart.

Hart told us Fritz had been with him since the early days and had appeared with him in nearly all his Westerns. He choked up as he told a few tales of their movie-making adventures. At the end of the last story, he turned to face the big monument, swept off his hat with a flourish, and bowed his head. He leaned with a hand against the bronze plaque and stood like that for half a minute or more.

Afterward we walked back up the hill in silence, and Dusty and I took our leave and climbed into my car. Gal was nowhere to be seen. As I swung the wheel and pointed us back down the hill, I saw Hart standing well away from the house with his face turned up to the sun just a little, facing out over the wide vista beyond his hilltop perch. Maybe he was just enjoying the warm sunshine. Maybe it was the impressive view of his private wilderness and the city below and far beyond it. Or maybe he was looking back through the years and seeing ghosts from the past—watching a lone cowboy out there somewhere, picking his way through the sagebrush with only his loyal pony for company. Something in me hoped it was that.

Chapter Three

"So, what did you think of 'ol Bill?" Dusty asked from under his hat as we drove back from the ranch. The question caught me by surprise. I'd thought he was napping as usual.

"Interesting bird. Not what I expected, I guess."

"Yeah," Dusty said. "He wasn't really puttin' on the dog today. Dependin' on who he's talking to about what, he can sound like the educated fellow from New York that he is, or he can lay on the cowboy lingo so think he makes *me* sound like a college professor." He sat up straighter and tipped his hat back. "So, what about your lumber case now?"

"I've got a guy I can call in Burbank. Another p.i. who owes me a favor. I'll hand it off to him."

"How do you plan to go about findin' this painting?"

"First thing, I need to find out all I can about Ty Jones. All I know is what I've read in the papers. You know much about the guy? Where he lived, where he came from, who his friends were?"

"No, he was just a fella I saw around the sets, or at the bar, like most of these drifters that float in and out of pictures. I doubt we've ever said more than a dozen words to each other. As far as friends, I couldn't tell you. He always seemed to sort of keep to himself. Hell, the best person to talk to would probably be Leo Rust."

"Talk to the guy who shot him?"

"They were more or less friendly, going back a ways."

"What changed?"

"Jones was paying a bit too much attention to Rust's missus. At least that's

CHAPTER THREE

how the boys tell it."

"Yeah, I remember reading that. Sounds like maybe I need to talk to both Rusts, then. Do you know where *they* live?"

"Him I do. Her—couldn't tell you. She walked out on him after the shooting."

"Think he'd talk to me?"

"Can't think why not, if he knows he's helping you prove Jones was a bad 'un. I doubt you'll like him much, though. He's maybe played the heavy in one too many movies—carries on like he's a real tough hombre, but it's all for show. He can be a surly sort."

"So can I. Let's go look him up, then."

"Drop me off at the bar, then you go." I gave him a look. "Until things simmer down, I need to steer wide of Leo for a bit. The boys would take it wrong if I was seen at his place."

"Didn't figure you much gave a damn what they thought."

"No, but there's Pooter to consider. I'm doin' what I can to keep peace in the valley."

***

There's not a man alive who couldn't have his character improved by having his ass kicked once in his life. Some should be on the monthly plan. Before I'd spent five minutes with him, I could see Leo Rust was one of those.

He lived just north of Whittier Boulevard in a part of East Los Angeles known as Belvedere Gardens. Much of it looked like the Hoovervilles of a few years back—makeshift houses cobbled together from chicken coops and scrap lumber, or tar paper and tin cans. Rust lived in an apartment court, old and run down but better than most of the housing in the area.

"So who the hell are you?" That was the greeting I got when he answered my polite knock on his apartment door. He looked me up and down with distaste. "If you're here about the telephone bill, go ahead and shut the damn thing off if you want. Then you can go pester someone else."

Besides the sunny disposition, I could see why they always cast him as the heavy. He had coal-black eyes under thick brows, a nose that had been broken a time or two, and a twisted upper lip that gave him a permanent sneer. He looked the part.

Explaining who I was and offering him a business card didn't improve his mood.

"You're here about Ty Jones, then. Listen, mister, the District Attorney ain't filing no case on me, so I got nothin' to say to no tin can copper. Here." He flicked the card at my face. It bounced off my hat brim and fluttered to the dingy doormat. "You can stick that up your ass and go crawl back in your hole." He started to shut the door, but I braced a palm against it and stiff-armed it back open. The flash of panic in his eyes told me Dusty was right. Like the cowboys put it, the guy was all hat, no cattle.

"What the hell you want?" He meant it to sound menacing, but I knew it was all bluff and was pretty sure that he knew I knew.

"Easy, pal. You're right. I *am* here to talk about Ty Jones." Before he could protest, I added, "Not about the shooting. A whole other matter." I looked around me. "But I'd rather not do business out here in the courtyard. Okay if I come in?"

He worked his mouth back and forth in indecision for a moment then pushed the door open wide and moved aside with a sigh. I retrieved my card from the mat and stepped in.

The room was small, and the air in it felt thick and slightly sticky, rank with sweat and tobacco smoke. Rust jerked his chin at a scuffed wooden chair while he took a seat on a sprung sofa. He picked up a half-filled whiskey glass from a side table and took a sip. He didn't offer me anything.

I spun the chair around and straddled it, crossing my arms on the back. We sized each other up for a good five seconds before he spoke.

"Well, spit it out. What's this all about, and why the hell should I talk to you anyway?"

"I'm looking into some shady business Jones might have been involved with." His eyes showed their first sign of interest. I stopped the question before he could ask it. "I can't say what, but I need to know a little about the guy. And I was told you could fill me in, that you two used to be tight."

CHAPTER THREE

"Used to." He snorted. "That's how I'd put it. We worked a lot of pictures together; drank a lot of whiskey together, if you want to call that *tight*. What the hell do you expect from me, anyhow? His life's history? Cause I don't know nothin' about that. I know he's done time, but I don't know where or why. I know he could be one mean bastard when he was drinkin', and he generally was. I know he was half Italian, half Irish, and a whole son of a bitch."

"I'm just after basics for now. Where did he live? Who'd he pal around with? That kind of stuff."

"Where he was livin' I don't know. He never stayed in one place for long. Couldn't tell you about no friends, neither. Hell, I could barely stand him back when we palled around. Doubt you'll find he had any other friends." His face darkened. "Unless you count my wife."

"Where do I find her?"

"Couldn't tell you, and don't give a shit. Try combin' the whorehouses, and you might run across her. It's where she belongs, the bitch." He knocked back the last of his whiskey in one angry gulp and refilled the glass to the rim.

It was pretty clear talking to this bird was a waste of time. I asked if he wanted me to relay any message when I spoke to his wife. He gave me one, but it would likely get me arrested, if not shot. I dropped the card on the table next to him and left him to his whiskey.

* * *

You couldn't call Queenan and me friends, but we operated on a sort of unspoken agreement. Neither of us thought much of the other's racket, but for a copper he was reasonably honest, and we'd been useful to one another in the past. So we'd cooperate with each other, to a point. Today, I was hoping the points were in my favor.

When I tapped on his door frame, he looked up from some documents, snatched off a pair of tortoiseshell glasses, and shoved them under the stack of papers in front of him. I'd heard that he'd lately had to shelve his vanity and start wearing cheaters, but I'd never yet caught him at it. It brightened my morning a little.

"You know, Ross, you could call ahead before you just come breezin' in here." He sounded more cranky than normal—probably trying to cover his embarrassment. He waved a beefy hand over the file stacks on his desk. "I'm a busy guy, you know. My caseload don't leave me a lot of time for entertaining."

"Sorry, Cap. I'll book an appointment with your social secretary next time."

"*Blah.*" The big hand slashed at the air. "The damage is done. Sit down and give me the bad news. What is it this time?"

I took a seat and perched my hat on my knee. I pointed at the half-hidden glasses. "You ought to wear those all the time. Makes you look like a guy who might have half a brain."

"Kiss my hairy ass. I'll ask again—what do you want?"

"Just looking for a little information on Ty Jones."

"Ah, the Gunfight at Griffith Park Corral." He chuckled at his joke and shook his big head. "You know I can't give you nothin' on that. Open case."

"I heard you'd closed it."

He shook his head again., "The D.A. refused to file—for now. That don't mean it's dead in the water. We may pin murder on this Rust character yet." He sat forward and gave me the hard eye. "And we don't need no private badges pokin' around in it in the meantime. If I hear you're so much as—"

I held up a hand. "I'm not looking into the shooting. Never fear."

He wasn't convinced. "Then what?"

"Looks like Jones may have been moonlighting from his cowboy gig. I'm running down a theft, and his name came up."

"Runnin' down a theft of what? From where? For who?"

"Come on, Cap. You know I can't give that out."

He snorted. "Of course, you can't. But you waltz in here like a damned ballerina and expect me to just open my files up to you. You got some real nerve, pal, you know that?"

I rotated my hat on my knee and choked back the urge to point out that ballerinas didn't usually waltz. It wouldn't help my case any.

"Look," I said, "I came in here to let you know I'm looking into the guy, so

CHAPTER THREE

you wouldn't think I was sneaking around behind your back."

"And...?"

"And to get your okay to look his place over."

He smacked his desk. "*There's* the cherry!"

"Give me credit, Cap. At least I asked first. And I'll owe you one."

Although we traded favors regularly, at present the books were dead even. I knew he wouldn't pass up a chance to hold my marker. He lit a cigar and gave me the dog eye for about ten seconds. "And Leo Rust don't figure into this caper of yours?"

"Not as far as I know. If it turns out different, I'll clue you in. I give you my word."

"Your word. *Blah*. I know what that's worth. You'll give me your scalp if I find out you're lying to me about any of this."

"Fair enough. Can you just give me Jones's address for now?"

"Rosslyn Hotel, room 515." When I got up to leave, he added, "Just remember—you don't break, and you don't take."

* * *

I left homicide and drove straight to the Rosslyn, over at 5th and Main. It wasn't the fanciest hotel in L.A., but it seemed pretty swanky for a bit part cowpoke. It wasn't every joint in town that had a neon sign on its roof you could have seen from the moon. But if Hart was right, then Jones hadn't been living off the peanuts he made as a day player.

I didn't know the house dick, but figured I'd better play nice, so I stopped at the desk and asked them to call him up. It wasn't a minute before I heard a voice close behind me.

"I gotta be dreaming here."

I turned around to find Dickie Benbow standing there. Dickie had been a graybeard with L.A.P.D. back when I was with the sheriff's department, and I'd have bet money he was long dead. But there he stood, older but looking fit enough for his years. In his snazzy three-piece pinstripe and straw boater, he looked like old man Doheny himself. It made me wonder if *he* was living off more than his police pension and what he made here rattling doorknobs and playing morality cop. I wasn't going to ask.

"Long time, Dickie. I had no idea you were working here."

He nodded. "Four years come March." He'd always been a guy of few words, but I wasn't sure there wasn't more to his curt reply. Since I'd helped put away a few bad apples from his department—and mine—several years back, I was less than popular with most of the cops in town. It was getting better as time passed and new faces came on the job, but a lot of the old-timers like Dickie still nursed a grudge.

Before I could get a read or decide how to play this if Dickie told me to go piss up a rope, he jerked his head to the side.

"Let's go this way." I was sure he was about to show me the bricks, but instead, he led me past the entrance and into the hotel's lounge. We took seats in a corner booth as a waiter stepped up.

"Hiya, Steve," Dickie said. He looked over at me. "Bourbon?" I just nodded, and he turned back to the waiter. "Four Roses, times two." He held up two fingers and winked at his joke, and the waiter drifted off.

"I figure you gotta be here on business," Dickie said. "And that punk at the front desk has big ears." He took off the boater and set it on the table like it was made of glass. "Anyways, I don't pay for drinks here. Side benefit of the job."

Steve brought our drinks and went away again. I hadn't touched my glass yet when Dickie clinked his against it.

"To better days," he said and took a sip. I picked mine up and took a swallow while Dickie's calm grey eyes studied me. "I can guess what's going through your head, Ross. Let me put your mind at ease. Far as I'm concerned, those boys back then all knew the game they were playing. If it hadn't been you, it would have been somebody else. You and me are jake."

I could see he meant it. "I appreciate that."

"So, that out of the way, what brings you to my sandbox?"

Without giving specifics, I told him I suspected Ty Jones had stolen something of value and I was looking for it, or for any clue where it might be.

"So you want to look the room over?"

CHAPTER THREE

"If I can. That is, if his stuff is still there."

"Oh, yeah. It's all there. We're under orders from the department and D.A.'s men to leave it alone until they give us the okey-doke. Hotel manager's fit to be tied." He blew out his cheeks. "But that being the case, I'm not sure I can—"

I stopped him. "I just came from Queenan. He knew I was headed here and why. And all he told me was 'Don't break, don't take.'"

He eyed me for a moment, then grunted and laughed. "That sounds about like Carl." He took a deep drink of bourbon. "Aw, what's the harm? As long as you don't mind having me for company."

"Okay by me."

* * *

We rode the elevator up to the fifth floor and when the kid running it opened the door, a woman was standing there, waiting. Dickie had started out but checked himself and stepped back to let her enter the car. She was youngish, dark-haired, pretty enough, but not show pretty. Maybe if she'd been less plainly dressed. She wore a nondescript brown dress that seemed designed to make her blend into a crowd, along with a pair of dainty white gloves. She seemed to be the shy type—she didn't speak or make eye contact with any of the three of us, almost like we weren't even there.

"Miss." Dickie gave her a professional smile and tipped his hat, but she gave no sign she noticed. He and I stepped out of the car, and as the doors closed I heard her say to the operator in almost a whisper, "Lobby, please."

Dickie stood and stared at the closed doors for a second.

"What's the matter?" I asked. "Never had a dame give you the freeze before?"

"It ain't that. Part of my job's knowing the ones that belong here and them that don't. She don't look like the usual floozy that drifts in, that's all."

"Not dressed like that."

He shrugged. "Ah, probably just somebody's sister visiting. I'll check with the kid in the elevator when we're all done here."

We went three doors down and stopped in front of 515. It had a *Keep out by order of the Los Angeles Police Department* notice taped to it. Dickie pulled out a ring of keys, singled out the passkey, and opened the door.

"What in holy hell?"

The room was in a shambles. Furniture upended, upholstery slashed, and stuffing pulled out and scattered, cabinet doors and drawers hanging open, their contents spread all over the floor. The closet had been emptied, and the clothing tossed on the bed and floor. There wasn't a lot, but every piece had pockets turned out, and many had seams ripped open.

I'd known the cops to leave a place in a hell of a mess after a search, but never anything like this. Somebody else had clearly been after something Jones had, or that they thought he had. Something small, so it wasn't Hart's painting, The place was in such a mess there was no way to tell whether they'd found what they were after.

"That dame," Dickie said, smacking a palm against his leg. "I knew there was something screwy about her." He left me there to look around while he went to talk to the elevator operator.

I sifted through the mess, not sure what I was looking for or even whether there was anything left to find. The girl, if it was her, had been thorough. She'd even pried the heels off a pair of boots I found next to the bed.

I did find one item of interest. Hanging askew over the footboard of the bed, half concealed under a filthy-looking shirt, was a pair of leather chaps. They were well worn, and down each leg they had a row of silver conchos identical to the one Hart had given me. At the bottom of the right leg there was no concho, just a couple of small holes connected by a tear in the leather where the decoration had been torn loose.

So Hart was onto the right bird, it seemed. That was worth knowing, at least. While I was looking through some papers in a pulled-out drawer, mostly check stubs from one Poverty Row studio or another, Dickie came back.

"Jimmy said he ran her up here about two hours ago. Never seen her before but didn't pay her much mind. No conversation on the way up, she just gave him the floor number. He did see her pull a key from her bag after she got

CHAPTER THREE

off. No hotel tag, so if it was a room key, it was a bootleg. You find what you were after?"

"No, but I pretty much confirmed that Jones was dirty. It's a start, I guess."

"I'm going to have to call Queenan," he said with an apologetic shrug. "He'll need to hear about this."

"Fine by me. At least if you make the call, he'll know not to blame this mess on me." I thanked Dickie for his help and left him a card. He promised to call if the woman was spotted coming around again. I doubted she would be. She'd either gotten what she was after or would start looking somewhere else.

Chapter Four

I headed back to the office to check on Monte. I took him for a break out back then we crossed the little gravel parking lot to Gus's diner for some dinner.

Benjy was sitting in an empty booth near the door, his nose in the *Times*. "Hiya, Benjy." I paused in the doorway, Monte at my heels. "Is Gus around?" Gus Karavolos, the owner, wasn't big on dogs in his place. Since he was also my landlord, I tried to stay on his good side.

Benjy looked up from his paper. "No, he took Aunt Sophia to the beach for the day. Bring him on in—the coast is clear."

I ate a quick soup and sandwich, and Benjy brought Monte a hamburger patty. I asked if I could leave Monte with him for a while the next day.

"You bet." He stroked the dog's furry head, "Always glad to have my old buddy visit."

"You sure the customers won't mind?"

"The people that come in here?" He waved a hand. "The regulars all know him anyway. He's a popular guy."

"Okay, thanks, pal." I tugged one of Monte's ears. "Let's go home, buster."

* * *

Before heading home, I went back upstairs to the office. I thought I'd better call and check in with Dickie Benbow.

"How'd Queenan take the news?" I asked him. "Hope you didn't get too much of an ass-chewing."

CHAPTER FOUR

"Nah, I got plenty of ass left," Dickie said. "I told him we kept the place locked up tight and watched as best we could. It ain't like we could post a guard on the door. He's sending someone over to check for prints, just to cover bases."

I didn't figure they'd find anything too useful, but it couldn't hurt to look. For all his faults—and he had plenty—Queenan was a thorough guy.

Dickie said nobody else he talked to had noticed the woman from the elevator or knew who she might be. To me, that made it pretty certain she was the one who had tossed the room—one of them, anyway.

I rang off with Dickie and was about to head out when the phone rang. I grabbed it up.

"Nate Ross."

"Nate, this is Bill Hart." He sounded agitated, a little breathless. Before I could ask what was up, he went on. "I just received another ransom note."

"Another one?" I'd had my doubts that Jones had been working alone. The typical ransom drop generally took at least two people—one to watch that the drop was made, and one to look out for cops and to be sure the victim was well away when the money was picked up. "Same kind of note?"

"Well, it says essentially the same thing, except that this one is typewritten."

"Same drop location?"

"Yes. Tonight, at midnight."

"Okay, hold on to it. I've got a couple of things to do, and then I'll head out to your place."

"I'll be waiting."

* * *

I drove with Monte over to the Buscadero. Pooter was tending bar. As usual, there were a few cowboys lounging around, and the mood seemed friendly, so they must have all been either pro-Rust or pro-Jones. Dusty was nowhere in sight. Pooter told me he was taking a deposit to the bank but would be back shortly.

While I waited, I borrowed the bar's office phone to call Queenan. He sounded less irritated than usual to hear from me. I took that as a good sign. Still, he couldn't resist the razoo.

"Why is it," he grumbled, "that the second Nate Ross comes on the scene, things start going haywire?"

"That room was turned upside down before I got there, Cap. Nothing to do with me."

"*Blah.* So you say. Seems like an awful coincidence. And you know where I stand on those."

"I do." To change the subject, and to get to the point I'd called about, I asked, "Your boys make any prints from it?"

"Nothing helpful so far. But Dickie said the dame was wearing gloves, so…"

"If it *was* her."

"Well, we talked to every resident and guest on that floor. Nobody admits having a visitor that fits that description, so it's a pretty good bet she's our baby. I don't guess you want to tell me what she was looking for?" There was an edge to the question.

"I would if I could. All I know is that it wasn't what I was looking for, for what it's worth." He answered that with a contemptuous grunt. "While we're talking about prints, though, I've got a question about the Rust shooting."

"Save it. I told you once already—open case."

"I'm not looking for any inside dope. Just wondering if your boys pulled prints from everyone on the set that day to compare with the one found on the brass in Rust's gun?"

There was a long silence. I knew he was deciding whether to tell me anything at all. I took it as a good sign that he didn't tell me straight off to go to hell.

"Of course we did," he said at last. "What do you think? We printed everyone who was still at the scene."

"*Still* at the scene?"

"Two guys, Stan Grange and Pete Chipman, had been sent to the stables earlier to pick up some horses, and the prop guy, Stovall, had vamoosed. But they all three had records for some petty mopery or other so we already had their prints on file. Not our boy. Why you askin' anyway?"

CHAPTER FOUR

"Just a thought. My theft caper likely involves someone besides Jones, and I could end up finding some prints on my end. But Leo Rust claims not to know of any friends of Jones's."

"You talked to Rust?"

"Only to try and get a line on Jones."

"Real charmer, that guy, ain't he?"

"Yeah, aces. You have anything on friends of Jones's?"

"I say again, open case. But no. So now, if you're through picking my pocket, I got plenty of other business to attend to."

"Sure, Cap. Thanks for the info."

"Yeah, yeah. Just don't you forget—if your little caper bumps up against mine, I need to hear about it. And I mean from you, not read it in the evening paper."

I promised and hung up. By the time I went back out to the bar, Pooter was sitting and talking with a couple of cowboys at a table near the back. He didn't appear to see me. Despite the bar's strict no-guns policy, I noticed a gun belt with a holstered pistol lying on the table. One of the cowboys, a youngster of twenty-two or so with dirty blonde hair, I'd seen in there a couple of times before. I didn't know his name, but the other guy was Joe Lopez. I knew Joe fairly well—he'd even helped me out on a case or two in the past.

Joe looked up and gave me a friendly wave as I took a seat at the bar. The two cowboys stood up, the kid bundled up the gun belt and tucked it under his arm, then he and Joe headed out the back door. I figured Pooter had just been reminding the guy about the rules, but before I could ask him about it, Dusty came back in.

Things still seemed a little frosty between him and Pooter. They exchanged a quick word or two, and Pooter disappeared into the back office. I filled Dusty in on my talk with Rust, finding Jones's room ransacked and the new demand Hart had received.

"So you were right," he said. "Sounds like Jones wasn't a lone operator."

"Apparently not. But Rust couldn't, or wouldn't, point me to any close friends. Claimed not to know anybody he ran around with regularly."

"Yeah, Ty was always kind of the stand-offish sort. Seemed to get along with the boys well enough, but I don't know you could call any of them his compadres." He laughed. "Even ol' Pooter didn't like him all that well. It's just that he hates Rust's guts and liver."

"I can understand that."

"What's your idea, then?"

"Well, I was hoping you could get away tonight. I could use an extra set of eyes and ears so it's not just me and Hart."

"I reckon Pooter won't mind closing the place on his own."

"I take it you two are back on speaking terms?"

"We've struck a truce, anyway."

"How about I come back for you around nine?"

"I'll be ready."

* * *

I drove home and grabbed a shower and a change of clothes, read the newspaper, and spent half an hour trying to find my binoculars. We headed back over to the Buscadero around eight-thirty. I took Monte along, not knowing who or what to expect at the ransom drop. The big mutt had better hearing and night vision than either of us, and could move faster, plus in my experience a lot of crooks who weren't fazed by guns would turn to butterscotch pudding at the sight of a big, snarling dog.

When I got to the Buscadero, they were having a busy evening. The cowboys had just been paid for the week's work and seemed determined to blow the whole kitty in one night. Still, Pooter assured Dusty and me that he could handle things. We climbed into my car to a little grumbling from Monte, who was not too happy about giving Dusty the front seat.

I was serenaded by the sound of the two of them snoring for nearly the whole drive to Hart's ranch. Hart met us at the door of the big casa again, still dressed in full cowboy garb. A swanky blue Packard touring car was parked in front of the house. It had to be Hart's buggy. Behind it sat a little gray coupe. Hart explained that it belonged to a nurse he'd called out because

CHAPTER FOUR

Mamie wasn't feeling well. I suspected that part of his concern for her was not knowing what we'd find waiting for us. He hadn't worried at the first drop, but maybe Jones's death changed things.

I left Monte in the car, and we all went up into the big living room again, where Hart showed me the new ransom note. Like he'd said on the phone, the wording was nearly identical to the first note, except that this one was typed. The drop instructions were the same.

"How shall we proceed then?" Hart asked. "I will defer to your expertise, Nate."

"Dusty and I will head up there in a few minutes," I said. "We'll pull off the road half a mile or so from the spot, then walk in until we're in sight of it. That'll put us there a good hour ahead of you and give us a chance to look things over. I'm guessing your party's going to arrive just enough ahead of time to make sure you come alone. We'll find a couple of good hiding spots, hopefully covering all escape routes."

"Do you think it likely we may encounter more than one person?"

"Tough to say. Me, I'd want someone else along, but I'm guessing Jones just had the one partner. And they might not want to cut anyone else in."

"And what would you have me do?"

"Exactly what the note says, nothing more or less. Let us manage the rest of it."

"Very well." He went over to his secretary, dropped the front, and took a big revolver out of a cubby hole. He spun the cylinder, checking the loads, then tucked it into his belt, underneath his jacket.

"I'm not sure you'll need that." I knew the old guy had handled guns plenty in his films, but movie and real-life gunplay were two different animals.

"I hope not," he said with a wry grin. "Still, as the man says, it's far better to have it and not need it than to need it and not have it."

I was tempted to argue the point, but figured if I were in his shoes, I'd feel the same way. I just hoped his moviemaking had taught him enough that he wouldn't end up shooting one of us.

* * *

Dusty and I drove the winding road up through Placerita Canyon. We were only a few miles more or less due east from Hart's place, so it was a quick trip. We didn't come across anyone else either coming or going on the lonely road. I pulled off to the side when Dusty, who was familiar with the area, judged we were about half a mile short of the Oak of the Golden Dream. We left my bucket tucked away in a little knot of trees in the shadow of the canyon wall. It was a near moonless night, so between the trees and the shadows, by the time we were twenty yards away, I couldn't see the car. I made note of a couple of landmarks to be sure we'd be able to find it on our way out.

We crossed the road in the shadow of some overhanging trees and worked our way slowly up along the other side. We'd dressed for the job. I had on dark pants and a black windbreaker jacket zipped up to the chin and wore a pair of rubber-soled shoes. Dusty, who led the way, was all in black, including his big Stetson. He looked like Hopalong Cassidy, except that in place of his usual boots, he was wearing a pair of knee-high moccasins. I'd taken the tags off Monte's collar, and he trotted silently along by my side.

When we'd picked our way along following the road for about ten minutes Dusty held up a hand and we stopped. He motioned me over and spoke in a low voice—whispers carrying further in the quiet. He pointed to a clearing fifty yards or so away. A big live oak with a squat, massive trunk and heavy limbs stretching their gnarled arms out in every direction stood alone in the scanty moonlight. I could just make out a large hollow in the heavy trunk, a gaping mouth opening on a space that looked big and deep enough to conceal a full-grown man. Or a cougar. Or a bear. The more I tried not to let my imagination drum up such thoughts, the more they came to me. I'd never been a fan of the wilderness.

"That's it?" I murmured.

"That's the one."

I wasn't sure what I had expected, but from the way Hart had talked about the site, I guess I pictured some sort of shrine, some impressive monument to an important happening in history. All I saw was a lonely, strange-looking tree with a few scattered boulders around it for company. Dusty quietly explained that Monte and I should stay there with a cluster of small trees for

CHAPTER FOUR

concealment. Meanwhile, he would work his way around to the far side and find a vantage point along the creek bed. We figured whoever planned to pick up the money would approach—or leave, on the off chance they were here already—either by way of the road or the creek.

He set off, and I settled in behind the divided trunks of a young sycamore. I braced my elbows in the fork of the thick trunks while I used binoculars to get a closer look at the big oak and to scan the area around it. The weak moonlight wasn't much help. Between the rocks and the wooded patches there were plenty of hiding places, but I didn't see signs of anyone else. I couldn't hear or see Dusty making his way to the opposite side of the clearing, but that was no surprise. This was his kind of game. After a long wait, I checked my watch and saw that it was only a few minutes until midnight. Monte sat patiently by my feet, and except for chewing on a hunk of the trees' sloughed-off bark—which I put a stop to with a nudge of my leg—he stayed quiet.

Except for the rustling of the breeze in the trees, a few stray crickets, and the distant wail of a coyote, the night was dead silent. Half an hour later, I was straining my ears and trying to decide if I could hear the soft gurgle of water when I picked up the sound of a car coming our way. Monte's ears were already up—of course, he'd heard it long before I did. He questioned me with a look, and I gave his wide head a reassuring pat.

I had a view of the road, and in less than a minute I saw the smear of headlights along the craggy bank the road followed. Seconds later, the lights themselves appeared around the bend. I hunkered down behind the tree and pulled Monte in a little closer, just in case.

I recognized the big touring car as it pulled off the road on the canyon side and, with much grinding of gears, made a sweeping U-turn to pull off on the other side. I'd told Hart to make plenty of noise coming in, and he'd taken me at my word. He opened the door before setting the hand brake—a nice touch. The ratcheting sound, plus the slamming of the door, reverberated through the canyon.

Monte had watched the car with interest and snapped to full attention when he saw Hart get out. I laid a hand on his head to let him know everything was okay. We both tracked Hart as the old duffer made his way along the narrow little path that led to the gnarled oak. He carried the envelope tucked under his arm and walked with his head up, eyes front and back straight. No doubt he was trying to project a bit of his on-screen bravado. Whether that was for himself, Dusty and me, or whoever else might be out there watching, I didn't know.

When he reached the tree, Hart moved in without hesitation and stuck his arm shoulder deep into the hollow to deposit the envelope. I couldn't help breathing a sigh of relief that nothing sprang out to attack him or drag him inside. He drew his empty hand back, turned without looking around him, and marched back just the way he'd come, like a guy who had a job to do and couldn't give a damn who liked it or didn't.

He slammed the door nicely again, sending a fresh round of echoes through the night. He tortured the transmission some more, then tooled off back down the winding canyon road, leisurely as a Sunday drive.

I turned full attention back to the big oak. If the money was to be picked up this time, I didn't figure our mystery note writer would waste much time about it. Once the last traces of Hart's big twelve-cylinder faded away, the quiet returned with only the same few occasional night sounds, with the addition of an owl that seemed to spook the hell out of Monte.

Then began the part of stakeout work I had always hated. The see-sawing from boredom to anticipation, the long wait for something, anything, or—as often as not—*nothing*, to happen. It didn't seem to bother Monte. Maybe dogs are more naturally patient. But I started getting cramped and tired and bleary-eyed after what I thought was an hour or more but my watch claimed was only fifteen minutes.

As I was considering whether I ought to buy a new watch, the crickets stopped and Monte stood, ears up and a soft rumble in his chest. I shushed him and strained my own ears and eyes. After a few seconds, I heard a soft, stuttering sound that even this city boy recognized as the snort of a horse. It was impossible for me to pinpoint what direction it had come from. My canine companion was fixed on a dense clump of chaparral beyond and to the left of the oak and partly screening the creek bed. Trusting his superior

CHAPTER FOUR

hearing, I trained my binoculars on that area and adjusted focus in time to see part of the chaparral move.

I quieted Monte again as a figure emerged from among the foliage. A slightly built guy, not very tall, dressed in a work shirt, dungarees, and a battered hat that shaded his face from view. He stepped clear of the chaparral and crept toward the big oak little by little, looking all around him as he went like he expected to be pounced on any second.

I had no doubt Dusty was on this guy, too. He'd come in from further along the creek than where Dusty had told me he would be, but he could hardly have gone unnoticed.

When the guy got within twenty yards or so of the tree, I started moving his way, with Monte trailing behind me. I kept my head low and stayed in the cover of the trees as best I could. When we had crossed half the distance, I caught a flicker of Dusty's silhouette coming from the creek bed. He was much closer than we were and, being more in his element than I was, was moving faster.

Our party guest reached the tree and, with one last look all around, half disappeared into the trunk's hollow. He emerged with the money envelope, checked inside it, then shoved it inside his shirt. I was still fifty feet away when I saw Dusty step out of the shadows and heard the sharp clicks as he drew back the hammer of his big Colt.

"Don't you move." Instead of heeding Dusty's stern order, our friend spun around and ran for the chaparral, speedy and true as the mechanical rabbit on a greyhound track.

"Monte, go!" I yelled while Dusty and I took off in pursuit. The big mutt streaked by me and made straight for the temporary gap made by our lamster crashing through the brush. Dusty reached the chaparral seconds before I did. I plunged after him through the thick scrub brush, and we came out almost together on the other side.

Our fleet-footed felon was thirty yards down the creek bank and had just reached a horse loosely tied there. Monte was coming on fast, but not fast enough if that horse got moving. I was silently cursing Dusty for making his move before either of us was close enough to put the arm on our grifter. The little guy untied the reins and made a smooth leap into the saddle that would have made old Bill Hart proud.

He yanked the reins around and let out a high-pitched "Yaah!" but the big animal only did a clumsy sidestep and turned to give its rider a confused look. By that time, Monte had closed in, and the big red dog launched like an archer's arrow. His full eighty pounds hit the startled horseman right in the breadbasket and carried him clean out of the saddle. The two of them came down in a tangled heap on the horse's offside. The guy started frantically groping around for something on the ground, but stopped and gave out a terrified wail when the dog scrambled to his feet and showed his fangs with a menacing growl. Dusty and I caught up in time for me to pull Monte off and prevent any bloodshed.

While I was getting Monte settled down, Dusty picked up what the errant art lover had been looking for—a .32 automatic. He pocketed it, dragged the little guy to his cowboy-booted feet, and got a pointy-toed kick in the shins for his trouble. He howled, shook the struggling little desperado by the arm, and was drawing back to deliver a good belt across the chops when the battered hat fell off, and a mass of long brunette hair tumbled out from underneath.

"What the hell?" Dusty's hand froze in mid-backhand. "He's a girl!"

And she clearly was. With a voice like an angry cat trying to scramble up a chalkboard.

"Let go of me, you Okie bastard," the thrashing little hellcat screeched. "I'll bite your damn ear off!" She moved as if to do just that and might have if Dusty hadn't given her another good shake.

"You best simmer down, missy." He pointed at Monte. "That one there's got bigger teeth than you do. Maybe I'd never strike no woman, but I doubt he's got my scruples."

She stopped tugging and squirming and stood breathing hard through her nose and looking at both of us with hot, angry eyes.

I took advantage of the pause to ask Dusty, "Why the hell did you call out so soon? We damned near lost her."

Dusty's teeth showed under his big mustache. "That horse wasn't going

CHAPTER FOUR

nowhere. Look at her back feet."

I looked at the big brown horse, who stood clipping at brush and watching us with only mild curiosity, and saw a leather strap stretched tight between the rear feet.

"While Belle Starr here was makin' her way through the scrub," Dusty said, "I tiptoed down here and hobbled her mare." He laughed. "Used a latigo string off her own saddle."

As he looked at our prisoner in triumph, his face changed. "Hold on, now." Still clutching her by the elbow, he half dragged her from the shadow of the trees into the faint moonlight. "Hell, I know you. You're Hazel Rust!"

Seeing her more clearly in the dim light, I recognized her, too. She was the dolly I'd seen getting on the elevator outside Ty Jones's hotel room.

Chapter Five

We traveled back to Hart's in my car. Hazel, who had promised to behave if I didn't handcuff her, sat in back. Dusty shared the back, just in case, and Monte rode in his accustomed place on the front passenger side. Dusty had tied Hazel's reins to a sturdy tree, and we'd left the horse still calmly grazing by the creek.

The ride back was nice and quiet. Hazel stared out the window most of the way while Dusty stayed alert for any hijinks. Monte slept. Me, I drove, and just to have some sound I turned on the radio. It was hard to get a signal in the canyon, but I managed to find a station playing a Jimmy Wakely tune I'd heard at the Buscadero.

Pulling up in front of Hart's home, we unloaded. Hazel still didn't speak but looked up at the big house in wonder and with a fair dose of apprehension. Hart had said he'd wait up for our report, but he obviously hadn't expected us to show back up with the culprit—let alone a woman—in tow.

Being quite an animal lover, Hart made no objection to Monte's accompanying us inside. I thought he might prevent any shenanigans on Hazel's part. She didn't seem particularly intimidated by Dusty or me, but kept a constant, wary eye on my dog. Hart explained that Gal was upstairs, asleep in her own room. A dog with a private bedroom—I hoped Monte wouldn't start getting ideas. We took our party into the sizable dining room so as not to disturb Hart's sister, who was also asleep upstairs.

"If you all can handle this without me," Dusty said as we led the girl in, "I'd like to go back for that mare. Can't leave her tied out there all night." Hart told him there was a ranch truck and a one-horse trailer behind the

CHAPTER FIVE

bunkhouse, down past the tower. He fetched the keys for him, and Dusty set off.

Hazel watched Hart closely. Whether she was feeling guilty or starstruck, I couldn't tell. Ever the gentleman, he treated her with the utmost courtesy, even though we made it plain we'd caught her dead-bang to rights. There wasn't much conversation until he had supplied each of us, even the girl, with a cup of coffee, and we were all seated around the big table.

I sized Hazel up for a long while. I'd thought she was pretty enough when I'd briefly seen her at the Rosslyn, but here in the soft light of Hart's dining room, even in her mannish attire, I could see why Rust worried about foxes in the hen house. I was trying to get a read, to figure how to play her, but I was also hoping my stare made her uneasy, maybe a little more likely to fold under questioning. It seemed to be working—she was fidgeting, shifting her eyes, biting her lip. I let her sweat under my steady gaze for fifteen or twenty seconds before I decided to start the party.

"Where's the painting?" I asked in my sternest Nate Ross, don't-fool-with-me tone.

"Painting?" It came out in a soft, almost juvenile voice. Nothing like the harpy shrieks we'd gotten from her in the canyon.

So it was going to be that way. "Look, sister." I glanced at Hart, then pinned her once more with my seal browns. "You'd better consider your position here. You're looking at some serious charges for this little caper of yours. Extortion alone will buy you five years in Tehachapi."

"Extortion?" Same kittenish tone. "I don't understand what you're asking me. I was just out for a nighttime ride and—"

"Knock it off, baby." I was losing patience fast. "That envelope you've got says different."

Her face reddened and she put a hand to her chest. "I don't have anything."

I couldn't resist smiling. "Did I say where?" Her eyes flashed fear, and the hand dropped. I held out a hand, palm up. "Let's have it."

Now, she tried a petulant tone. "Mister, I told you I don't know what you're talking about."

"Here's the deal, and think fast because I'm only giving you this one chance."

I lifted the hand a little higher. "You fish it out, or I will." She hesitated, and I added, "Don't kid yourself that I'm not that kind of guy."

She bought the bluff. "Oh, all right. But turn around first."

Hart did an immediate quarter turn in his seat and looked away.

"Nothing doing," I told her. "For all I know, you've got another little popgun tucked away. Give. Now."

She looked murder at me, undid the top two buttons of her shirt, and slid out the brown envelope. Without taking her glare off me, she slapped the envelope on the table. She refastened one of the buttons but left the top one undone. Guess she figured if nothing else worked she might be able to hoochie-coochie herself out of her fix. I slid the envelope over to Hart, who was still averting his gaze.

"It's safe to look now, Bill." I told him to make sure his cash was all there. He checked inside the envelope and nodded that it was.

"All right, then." I turned back to Hazel. "Mr. Hart's got his money back. Now tell me where we can find his painting."

She looked at the two of us in turn. If the loose button wasn't going to work, she'd try for sympathy. And she pulled out all the stops. Trembling lower lip, wringing hands, wide, frightened eyes. When she spoke, she put just the right quiver in her voice.

"I don't know. I swear I don't." I could see that Hart was already weakening. When I didn't budge, she decided to go for broke. "You have to believe me!" she wailed, then turned on the full weeps. It wasn't going to win her any Oscars, but it wasn't a half-bad performance, in a community theater kind of way. She buried her face in her crossed arms on the table, her shoulders heaved, and she broke up her animal howls with plenty of gasps and snuffling noises. When she raised her face, her eyes were pinched shut, and her mouth was twisted in pure agony. She had it all, except for one thing.

"We get the idea, angel," I said. "But if you really expect to sell it, you've got to learn to squeeze out a tear or two. Dry eyes don't cut the mustard."

She was determined, though, and kept up the routine until I slapped a palm down hard on the table. "Enough of that; you're not Bette Davis!" I barked at her. "And I'm getting bored with it already."

CHAPTER FIVE

The act stopped at once. She sat up straight and fixed me with the same death stare she'd given us up in the canyon.

"What are you, made of stone, you son of a bitch?"

Hart actually gasped, and I had the idea that maybe he'd never heard a woman swear before. Looked like we really did travel in different circles.

"It's late, and I'm not in the mood for games," I told her. "You don't want to give up the painting, just say so and I'll hand you off to the police. You can try your crying bit out on them. I'll warn you, though, I hear those lady coppers can swing a blackjack just as hard as the boys can."

"I tell you, I don't know where that painting is. God knows, I wish I did."

"If that's so, who does know? Now's not the time to hold out."

"Nobody knew but Ty. He played it cagey—he wouldn't trust...me."

I grinned at her. "You said 'me,' but you were about to say 'us.' Who else is in this little comedy routine?"

She took a sudden interest in the tablecloth. I let her think it over for a while before I spoke again.

"Believe it or not, sis, we're trying to do this thing without bringing any cops into it. But it's all up to you. Once I give you over to them, it's their party, and they might not even care who your playmates are. A bird in the hand and all that."

"There was just Pete." She looked up. "Pete Chipman."

The name rang a bell in the back of my mind. Chipman. It took a minute, but then I had it. Pete Chipman was the name of one of the missing cowboys Queenan had mentioned. The ones who had left the movie set before Jones was shot.

"And how does he figure in all this?"

"He was Ty's partner."

"In what?"

"They were dealing in goods. Pete knew people who collected stuff." She looked around the room. "This kind of stuff. People who would pay top dollar and didn't care where it came from."

"They were pulling burglaries?"

"Sometimes. Not always. They took stuff from the studios, from prop rooms. Sometimes from sets they worked on. A house once in a while. Guns, mostly. But saddles and other stuff. Now and then, they'd spot something they knew they'd have a buyer for, and they'd line up the buyer and then come back for it later. No rough stuff. Just pull a sneak and grab it."

"Like they did here?"

"Yeah. This was supposed to be the big one. Pete said this painting was worth a mint."

"Five grand in ransom's not exactly what I'd call a mint."

"It wasn't supposed to happen like that. Pete said he had a big-money buyer. But he was playing it close—he wouldn't tell Ty who the buyer was. Afraid Ty would try and make the deal on his own, I guess. But him being so foxy, Ty started thinking Pete was just looking to cut him out. Plus, he was nervous—they'd never pinched anything this hot before. So Ty took the painting—they'd had it stashed at his place—and he hid it. He wouldn't say where, not even to me."

I knew she could be spinning us a yarn, but I'd seen enough to know she wasn't much of an actress.

"So what *were* you looking for in Jones's room?"

She turned her palms up. "Anything. Something that might tell me where the painting's at. It wasn't like Ty owned property, had any place he could have hid it out. And he wouldn't have trusted anybody else to hold it for him—they'd be sure to ask questions. So I thought maybe he'd checked it at a freight office, stashed it in a train station or bus station locker. If I could just find a claim check, a key, or whatever…"

"Well, you did a thorough toss, I'll give you that."

"That wasn't me. Well, it wasn't *all* me."

"How's that?"

"The place was already pretty well turned upside down when I got there."

"Chipman?"

"Who else?"

"So you figure he's got the painting now?"

"No, I know he doesn't."

"How come?"

CHAPTER FIVE

"Because he came to see me that same night. He had it in his head that maybe I had the painting, or at least that Ty had told me where it was. He wouldn't believe… he…" she choked back a sob, and her eyes welled up. Real tears this time.

Hart quickly looked away as she undid the second button on her shirt again and tugged the collar to one side. Just below her collarbone I saw three angry red marks, perfectly round, the skin blistered.

"He burned me," she said. "Pushed his cigarette against me to make me tell him where the painting was. But I didn't, because I couldn't." She buttoned herself back up and wiped her eyes with the back of a hand.

She gave Hart a pleading look. "That's why I sent you the note. I knew how Ty had worked it before, so I…I really wasn't trying to cheat you. I just needed a stake to get away, somewhere Pete wouldn't find me." She looked back at me. "He threatened me. He told me if I didn't come through, I might end up like Ty."

"Speaking of that," I said. "How does your husband figure into all this business?"

"Leo? He doesn't. He was no part of it. He didn't even get along with Ty after he found out…well…."

"Did he get along with Chipman?"

"He doesn't even know Pete that well. I mean, they've worked together, but other than that…"

I wasn't sure how much to believe her about Rust. Sure, she'd run out on the guy, but that didn't mean she would be willing to peach on him. Women can have a strange sense of loyalty. I decided to drop that line for the time being.

"Where would I find Chipman?"

"I don't know. Honest. He doesn't really live anywhere. He's moved around, bunked with one or another of the boys now and then. Mostly, he camps out in the hills by himself. He spends time at the Buscadero like they all do, but not since the shooting. Right now, he could be anywhere."

Just then, we heard the low rumble of an engine out front, and Hart went to open the door for Dusty. They came back in, and Dusty asked Hazel a few questions about the horse, starting with whose it was. He got from her that she had "borrowed" it from a barn at the Monogram Ranch, where several horses had been temporarily stabled for a film shoot in the morning. She said she had ridden the train up to Newhall from Union Station and taken a taxi from there out to the ranch.

While Dusty was talking to Hazel, I took Hart into the kitchen for a private conference. As I'd expected, he didn't want the girl turned over to the cops—I even had to talk him out of giving her some money. He had no intention of prosecuting, he said, and he felt she'd given me some helpful leads in looking for his missing portrait. Which was true enough, I supposed, assuming she wasn't selling us a fairy tale. I had my reservations about not letting the law take its course, but he was the client.

Hart said he would deliver the filched horse to the movie ranch later in the morning and that he was sure he could smooth things over. Dusty and I, meanwhile, would drive back with Hazel, who was staying at one of the low rent flops downtown. After that, I hoped to make it home ahead of the sunrise and, if I was lucky, get three or four hours of sleep.

I had a quiet drive back to the city as Hazel, Dusty—of course—and even my faithful dog, all slept almost from the moment we'd left Hart's ranch behind. I dropped Hazel at her hotel with one of my business cards and a promise from her to let me know if she saw or heard from Chipman. I had my doubts she'd keep her word.

It was nearly four a.m. when we got back to the Buscadero. Dusty had promised Pooter he would open in the morning, so he was planning to just nap in the office for a couple of hours. When I pulled up in front, we could see through the door glass that there was light coming from the back room.

"Dadgum knothead," Dusty muttered, "He bitches about the electric bill, but two out of three nights he leaves the damn office lights on." He fished out his keys as he got out of the car. "You want to come in for a snort?"

"No, thanks. I need some sleep."

"All right. You gonna be needin' me again tomorrow?" He looked at his watch. "Later today, that is."

"I'll let you know, pal. But listen, thanks for tonight."

CHAPTER FIVE

"Any time." He gave Monte a pat and shut the door.

Chapter Six

I woke up to Monte pawing at the side of the bed. The clock on my nightstand said 6:45.

"What's eating you, pal?" I tried to keep the annoyance out of my voice—he could be pretty sensitive—but I'd just let him out two hours earlier, so I couldn't see why he was so insistent. Then as my fog lifted a little, I noticed the phone was ringing. I was in the middle of a yawn, and it rang twice more before I grabbed it up. "Yeah?"

"Nate, it's Pooter." I'd never spoken to the guy before when he wasn't loud and cheerful, but the voice on the phone sounded weak and brittle.

"What's going on?"

"Dusty's been shot."

I came awake all at once and started firing off questions. Pooter explained that he'd gone to the Buscadero just before six—since he hadn't heard from Dusty, he wasn't sure Dusty would remember he was supposed to be there to open. He'd found the bar in a mess, and when he went into the office, the lights were on and there was a large pool of blood on the floor, with bloody drag marks leading to the walk-in cooler. He'd found Dusty lying on the cooler floor, unconscious, both hands clutching a bar towel against a bullet hole in his chest.

He'd called an ambulance and tried to revive Dusty but couldn't rouse him. They'd taken Dusty to the receiving hospital for emergency treatment. He had a punctured lung and major blood loss from the gunshot wound, and he had a serious concussion from receiving a nasty crack on the back of his head. Pooter didn't know any more yet—he was still waiting for Dusty to

CHAPTER SIX

come out of surgery.

I showered and dressed as quickly as I could and fed Monte a short breakfast. Mine could wait. I didn't want to waste time going to the office or diner, so I left the dog in the backyard. I'd be back for him as soon as I could. If he dug for gophers in the meantime, so be it.

My natural inclination was to rush to the hospital, but Pooter had said they hadn't given him any idea when Dusty would be out or if he'd be able to see him anytime soon. He told me they'd given him to understand that things looked pretty grim. I decided I'd be of more use to my old pal if I went to the Buscadero to see what I could learn. Whatever had happened, and whoever had done this, I needed to find out, pronto.

* * *

There was a police radio car along with a couple of detective cars parked in front of the bar when I rolled up. As I headed for the front door, a uniformed copper who was lounging against the patrol car tossed his cigarette and stepped in front of me on the sidewalk.

"Whoa, bub." He held up a palm. "Gotta go oil the tonsils someplace else. The bar's closed."

"Yeah, I know." I showed him my license. "Can you tell me who's running the show?"

He gave me the dog eye. Whether he recognized the name or was just suspicious of private eyes in general, I didn't know, or give a damn. Before he could tell me to get lost, a familiar, booming voice cut in.

"Yeah, I was wonderin' how long it'd be before you came sniffin' around." Queenan walked from the doorway to where we stood. "It's all right, Lonnie," he told the uniform. "I got this guy." He beckoned to me. "Come on." Lonnie gave me a last sour glance and went back to his fender as I followed Queenan inside.

Pooter hadn't exaggerated. Whoever had come in had gone through the place, top to bottom. Cabinets in the back bar were open, and their contents dragged out and scattered. Drawers had been pulled out, crates and boxes dumped, whole shelves of bottles and glassware swept onto the floor.

"Office is in pretty much the same shape," Queenan said. "I'd give you a peek, but the print boys are still workin' in there."

"What are you doing here, Cap? It's not like this is a homicide case." I managed to check myself before I added *yet*.

"Oh, it ain't mine. Local robbery dicks are on it, but when I heard who the victim was, I had to come look things over for myself."

"What do we know so far?"

He pushed his hat back on his big head, gave his hairline a scratch. "There ain't no *we*." His tone softened as much as he was capable of. "Look, Ross, I know you and Vanner are *simpatico*, but this is a police case. You muckin' around in it isn't gonna do your pal no good. We'll find our baby, I guarantee it."

"Yeah, okay, okay. So what do *you* know so far?"

He cleared his throat. He motioned to a table, and we sat. "Straight-up burglary, from the looks of it. Back door pried open, you can see how they went over the place—looking for cash, I guess. The partner, Barnes, said there was none on hand. Said he left the cash register drawer and the safe standin' open when he locked up. He took the day's receipts home to count 'em. The twenty bucks in bills and coin he left in the register wasn't touched. Maybe our guy couldn't be bothered with chump change. Barnes says he left around 2:30—Vanner must have come in sometime after that and walked right into it."

"It was just before four. He was helping me out with something, and I dropped him off here."

"Okay, good, that helps to know. You see anything that looked off when you were here?"

"I didn't come inside. The office lights were on. Dusty just thought it was his partner." It hadn't really struck me until then. "Shit. If only I *had* come in with him—."

"*Blah*. Don't start thinking like that, pal. For all you know, if you did, you'd both be in surgery now. Or worse." I knew he was right, but knowing it didn't make me feel any better. I tried to shake it off.

CHAPTER SIX

"Anything else?" I asked.

He spread his hands. "Afraid that's all the news that's fit to print for now. We ain't been here that long yet."

"Who do I talk to when you *do* know more?"

"The robbery guys are Deacon and Valverde. But you come straight to me on this one. I'll keep my ear in, and I'll share what I can. Fair enough?"

"I appreciate that, Cap." I stood to go. "Hey, before I forget…" I thought I'd better take advantage of his sympathetic mood. "Anything new on the Rust shooting?"

"Not much. We tracked down one of the cowboys who'd left the set and got his statement."

"Which one—Chipman?"

He paused, and I could see the wheels turning. Finally, he said, "No, the other one, Grange. He saw *nada*. Chipman's still in the wind. You know how it is—these damn cowboy extras are all about one step above hobos. Maybe one in ten of 'em has a fixed address."

"Well, happy hunting. And thanks again."

* * *

I was still a little fuzzy from too little sleep and my sudden wake-up, so I went back home to get Monte, and we drove to the office. I planned to grab breakfast and some sorely needed coffee at Gus's, then leave the dog in Benjy's charge so I could check on Dusty.

After I told him about Dusty, Benjy was even more happy to help. So after a quick bite and an extra cup, I left Monte there and went up to the office to check for mail and messages and to call the hospital. I rang the main desk and asked if there was a worried-looking cowboy type pacing in the waiting room. After a couple of minutes Pooter came on the line to tell me that Dusty was still in the operating room and there was no new report.

With nothing else to do until Dusty was out of surgery and I could find out more about what had happened, I decided to keep my mind occupied with my other case. So I headed over to pay Leo Rust another call. Hazel's story hadn't fully convinced me, and I wanted to see what Rust himself would have to say about Pete Chipman. If Jones really had double-crossed Chipman, I couldn't help but wonder if the falling-out between him and Rust might have been over something more than Hazel.

I wasn't sure if I'd find Rust at home, or if he'd picked up work for the day, but either way, I didn't figure to waste the trip. If he was here, I'd brace him about Chipman. If not, it would give me a chance to search his place. For all I knew, I might get lucky and find Hart's painting sitting in the closet.

I was crossing the street half a block away when a guy came out the front entrance of Rust's courtyard. He was short and stocky, with reddish, close-cropped hair, and was in bad need of a shave. He wasn't wearing the telltale hat, but the boots and high-cuffed dungarees were a giveaway. As a rule, the only cowboys you saw around town were movie cowboys. He glanced my way as he came down the two steps, then he headed the other direction and disappeared around the corner. I didn't think much about it. Rust likely wasn't the only day player living in such a place, and he still had plenty of amigos among the cowboy crowd.

I knocked several times on Rust's door but got no response. I put an ear to the door. Nothing. I was about to put my picks to work on the kid stuff lock when just for fun, I tried the knob, and it turned. I eased it open—it might be that Rust was in the small bathroom, but I didn't hear running water or other telltale sounds. When I'd come through the narrow entryway and into the room, I discovered that Rust was home all right. But he wasn't in the bathroom. He was stretched out crosswise across the pull-down bed, fully dressed, boots and all. When I came closer, I could see that he was very, very dead.

I went back to the doorway, took a quick look up and down the court, and closed the door again. I checked the body and saw two stab wounds below the ribs and just left of center. He hadn't been dead, I didn't estimate, for more than a few minutes. It had to have been the cowpoke I'd seen leaving. I went to a window that looked out onto the side street the guy had turned down, but there was nobody in sight. I knew I'd need to call the police on this, but I wanted to have a good look around first. There wasn't much to see.

CHAPTER SIX

Rust didn't have a lot, and his housekeeping wouldn't have won any ribbons, but I could still see that the place had been searched. Hart's painting was *not* in the closet, or anywhere else, and I didn't find anything to give me a clue where it might be.

My first thought was to place an anonymous call to the police. I was anxious to get to the hospital and see about Dusty, and I didn't relish wasting a couple of hours explaining myself to suspicious and hostile cops. But I was sure I'd just seen the killer, so they'd need what information I could give them. Rust didn't have a phone—apparently, they had disconnected it. I used the fly-specked directory tacked up next to the mailboxes to find the manager, who told me to buzz off until I explained that I needed his phone to report a dead man in apartment number four.

I sat on the steps out front and smoked until the car with the two bluesuits showed up. They gave me a minimum of grief, for a change, and after they'd looked things over one stayed at the door while the other—obviously the senior partner—stood out front and made bored chitchat with me.

Half an hour later, a big black Ford drove up and Queenan got out, along with a detective I thought maybe I'd seen a time or two but didn't know. The copper with me nodded to them as they came up the walk.

"Twice in one day. What mortal sin have I committed to deserve this?" Queenan shook his head and looked past me to where the other uniform stood guard.

"I was about to ask the same thing, Cap," I said. "I'm surprised to see you out in the sunshine. Again. Is the department budget so tight they've got to send captains out on calls now?"

"Nah, my big fanny ought to be back behind my desk, but when I hear Nate Ross has called in a hot one—or I guess I should say a *cold* one—what can a guy say? I can't help myself." He indicated the other detective. "Do you know Fred Grumman? Fred, this here's the famous Nate Ross."

"I've heard your name around, Ross." I got that same line a lot whenever I was introduced to cops, and I knew it could mean a lot of different things. But Grumman at least shook my hand—I didn't get much of that.

"So," Queenan said in a mock cheery voice, "Who's today's lucky lottery winner?"

I was going to have to tell him sometime. "Leo Rust."

His smile, if that was what it was supposed to be, vanished like smoke. He turned to Grumman.

"Fred, why don't you get the boys to show you what you got? I need to have a word or two with Ross here."

Grumman nodded and headed inside, along with the uniformed copper.

Queenan took his sweet time. He pulled out a fresh cigar and trimmed it with a pen knife. He touched a match to it and rotated it slowly in the flame, like meat on a spit. He knew that I knew what was coming, and he wanted to make me sweat. But I'd done this dance with him plenty of times before, and I knew all the steps by heart. Let the guy have his fun. I could wait.

He finished his little ritual and took a couple of puffs to get the cigar glowing a nice angry red before he spoke. When he did, his tone was calm. With him, that was never a good sign.

"I remember a conversation we had not too long ago," he said, looking out at the street, the trees, everywhere but at me, "Where you told me you weren't nosin' around my shooting case."

I started to answer, and still not looking at me, he held up a beefy paw. "You told me to my face that you didn't think the case you're workin' had anything to do with Leo Rust and that if you found out different, you would put me wise. You said—and I quote—'I give you my word.' Am I rememberin' things right so far?"

"Yeah, but—"

The big mitt came back up. "Save the *but*." He pointed at the building. "Now you're tellin' me the very party we discussed is in there feedin' the maggots. And I'm supposed to believe you were just talkin' to him about some bullshit theft?" He teased some more smoke out of his cigar. "I've cut you a lot of breaks in the past, Ross. Not because I like you—don't kid yourself—but because every now and then, usually without meaning it, you end up being useful. And because for a peeper, you're more or less honest, and I respect that."

He turned to look at me at last. His pig eyes went hard, and the red started

CHAPTER SIX

at his Adam's apple, working its way like a thermometer, slowly rising up past his eyebrows. "But I'm givin' you *my* word that if you try to tell me that now your little pissant theft caper don't have no connection to my case, I'm gonna do what I should have done the very first time you pulled a stunt like this." He jabbed a stubby forefinger at me, and his foghorn voice went high and raspy, like a revival preacher's, "I'm gonna lock your lyin', connivin' ass up for interferin' with a police investigation, and then I'll see about pullin' your p.i. ticket. If you're lucky, maybe you can get a job busing tables at the Brown Derby, where the most harm you can do is to maybe bust a dish or two."

He was huffing like an angry bull by the end of his tirade, and I seriously thought he might throw an aneurysm and croak on me then and there. I did my best to look chastised and contrite, hoping it would drop his blood pressure back into the low hundreds. Before I could think of something to say that wouldn't set him off on a fresh rant, he stopped panting and lost some of the lunatic glaze in his eyes. He took another couple drags on the cigar, and it seemed to calm him. When he spoke again, what came out was pretty close to his normal voice.

"All right, I've had my say. Now it's your turn. But you better choose your words wisely. No givin' me the song and dance—you ain't Bojangles Robinson."

"Okay, Cap. I'll admit that maybe I ought to have talked to you first, but I didn't know for sure that Rust figured into my case. The possibility only just came up, and I came here to try and see if there was anything to it. I didn't really think there was, I was just covering bases. I sure as hell didn't expect to walk into a murder. And as soon as I did, I called you boys up."

Queenan's eyes were locked on mine while I talked. He was ready to pounce at the first whiff of bullshit.

"I'm still not giving up my client." I paused, waiting for the objection, but he just continued staring at me. "But if it helps here, I'll tell you what I can." Without mentioning any names or locations, I told him about my client getting two ransom notes, the first one from Jones. I told him about Dusty and me staking out the drop and that it turned out to be Rust's wife who had sent the second note and who we'd caught making the pickup.

"This is the dame that was playing footsie with Jones?" Queenan asked.

"Right. She said Jones and Pete Chipman had a theft racket going."

That interested him. "Chipman—our missing cowboy."

"Yeah. And she claimed that Rust wasn't involved in any of it. Said he hardly knew Chipman. But I thought I'd better talk to Rust himself and see if I believed any of that. That's all I came here for."

Queenan nodded, chewing on all of this. "Okay. But you should have tipped me the minute Chipman's name came up. That's a definite connect to my case."

"Maybe so. But I figured if I put him and Rust together in this thing, I could possibly hand you two for one."

That got me the dog eye. "*That's* what you planned to do, was it?"

I started to answer, but he cut me off. "Maybe you better stop your story right there, for your own good. Right now, tell me about this guy you saw—the one you mentioned when you called this in."

After I described the cowboy I'd seen leaving the place, Queenan told me to follow him to his car. He pulled out a thick file, took a photo from it—a mug shot—and handed it to me.

"That our boy?"

I'd only had a quick look at the guy, but it was enough. The hair was a little longer in the picture, but it was the same face.

"That's him. Who is he?"

"Meet Pete Chipman."

"Yeah?" I studied the photo. The booking info on it showed the arrest date and charge. "Pinched for receiving back in '32. What was the story?"

"Prowl car pulled him and his brother over in Edendale for a busted taillight. Coppers smelled hooch in the car—and this was before repeal, remember—so the boys went through the heap and pulled a pint of gin out from under the seat. Then, under a rug in the back, they found a pile of swag that come from a recent home burg up in the hills. They booked the two of 'em for receiving, and the dicks tried to make 'em for the burglary, but the D.A. wouldn't file it, the pansy."

CHAPTER SIX

I held up the mugshot. "I don't suppose I could—"

"Keep it," he growled. "It's a spare." He stabbed me in the chest with his blunt finger. "But get this through your thick noggin. We want this bird for murder, not on some penny ante larceny beef. You get any hint of his whereabouts, you call me tout suite and step aside. Once we got him in custody, *maybe* if you're a good boy, I'll let you talk to him about lesser crimes. Am I clear on that?"

I tucked the photo away. "You'll be my first call."

"I'll be your *only* call, or you'll be talkin' to him from the same side of the bars." He bit down hard on what was left of his cigar and glared at me for emphasis.

"Understood."

"So how's Vanner doing, anyway?" he asked, in a sudden but welcome change of subject.

"Still in surgery, last I heard. I haven't made it over there yet." He looked surprised at that, and I motioned towards Rust's place. "I ran into a slight delay."

"The Nate Ross luck still holding."

"Yeah. Your boys turn up anything on that at the bar? Witnesses, prints?"

"Zilch on witnesses. But as far as prints…" He gave me a warning look. "This ain't for publication, you get me?"

"Whatever you say."

"Okay. Well, printing the bar you can guess was a waste of time. We'd only end up with hundreds of suspects. So the guys concentrated mainly on the office, especially the safe. Mostly Vanner's and Barnes' prints in there, of course, but we got a few others."

"Any i.d. on those?"

"No such luck. But they did make one very interesting find. See, turns out Vanner was shot with his own *pistola*—you know, that big old museum piece he packs around? Looks like our burglar was hiding out when Vanner came in, clocked him on the back of the head. With what we don't know—maybe with the pry bar they used on the door. Anyway, while he was down, I guess they got their hands on his gun. Then it looks like Vanner shook it off, and there was a tussle. The guy feeds Vanner one, spooks, and legs it out the way he came in. One of our boys found the hog leg in an ashcan halfway down the alley."

"Prints on it?"

"There's the interesting part. Thumbprint on it matches the one on that brass from the Ty Jones shooting."

"Son of a bitch. You get anywhere with *that* print yet?"

He shook his head. "Pinker and his lab guys have been digging deep in the files. Every known shooter, anybody connected with film work, every cowboy type we've ever so much as vagged for the night. *Nada* so far."

I was glad to hear Ray Pinker was personally involved. He headed up the crime lab; nobody was better with prints. "So now, I guess they've added known burglars to the mix."

"Right. Still no idea what our guy was lookin' for, though. According to Barnes, there's nothin' missing." He pushed his hat back, took a deep breath. He looked toward Rust's door, where we could hear Grumman directing one of the lab guys who was taking photos. "Funny, with this new wrinkle we were just about to pay Rust another visit, press him on any connections he might know of between any of these cowpunchers and burglaries. Anyway, looks like he don't have to worry no more about being tagged for Jones's murder."

"Yeah, I guess not."

"Maybe he'll even end up with a clean bill on that, if we can run down our mystery guest, not that it'll matters much to him." He opened the car door, dropped the file on the seat, and closed the door again. "Well, let's go on in. Sooner you give Grumman your statement, the sooner you can go see about Vanner."

Chapter Seven

Grumman had been thorough. I had to give them the whole story three times before he'd let me walk. By then, it was almost three o'clock. I drove straight to the Hollywood Receiving Hospital, only to find out that Dusty had been transferred to Queen of Angels, a mile from my office. Before heading over there, I dropped a nickel and called Benjy to make sure he wouldn't mind holding onto Monte a little longer. He said it was fine—Gus's gout had started acting up, so he would likely be home with his feet up for two or three days. Meanwhile, he said, he had Monte stashed in the small back office, gnawing on a soup bone, happy as a lark.

With the afternoon traffic, it took me nearly half an hour to get to Queen of Angels. I took it as a good sign that they'd transferred Dusty. I didn't know if that meant he'd be in any shape for visitors, but I still wanted to see for myself how he was doing.

I spoke to the nurse at the desk, who was younger and friendlier than the cranky battle axes they had at the receiving hospital. If it hadn't been for my hurry to see my pal—and the ring on her finger—I might have been tempted to prolong the conversation. Anyway, she told me that Dusty was doing okay, considering—that surgery had gone well, but that between the concussion and the heavy loss of blood, he was still unconscious.

I was as quiet as possible as I slipped into the room, even though it probably didn't matter much. I was surprised to see that Dusty wasn't alone. A man was standing beside the bed with his back to the door and me. He had one hand on Dusty's arm, and the other held his hat alongside his leg. Despite my soft entry, he looked over his shoulder at me. I couldn't place the face, but there was something sort of familiar about it. The guy was about my age, give or take. He was medium height with a compact build, clean-cut, and dressed in a neat gray serge suit with a colorful but not gaudy red and blue tie. I just figured he must be a doctor—maybe one of the surgeons dropping by to see how his work was holding up.

There was brief confusion in his eyes. Before I could say anything, he spoke.

"Good afternoon." There was a soft drawl in the voice. Not Deep South, but definitely not California. His eyes swept me top to bottom. "Are you a doctor?"

"I was about to ask you the same thing."

He gave me a closer look. "Are you with the police?"

"No." I made a vague gesture toward the bed. "Just a pal. And who might you be?"

He turned full around. His eyebrows crowded together with concern, maybe suspicion. "I'm—" The worried expression faded, and his eyes sparkled, as though he'd just figured out the answer to a riddle. "Of course—you're Nate Ross."

That frosted me a little. It started me thinking maybe he was a newshawk, sniffing around for a story. If so, I intended to toss him out on his keister.

"I know who I am," I said. "The question was, who are *you*?"

"I'm Walt. Walter VanNeer." He nodded toward the bed. *"Junior,* that is." He took a step forward and stuck out a hand. "I'm Dusty's son."

I shook the hand automatically while thoughts went ping-ponging around inside my head. VanNeer—Dusty's family name. Why'd he change it to Vanner? Somebody mispronouncing it. Rodeo announcers, that was it. Not important now. I looked at Dusty's son. Dusty's son. The familiar face. The voice.

I guess he caught the baffled look on my mug. If I had any doubts he was who he said, they faded as soon as he grinned. Dusty has this grin he gets when he's enjoying a joke at someone else's expense, usually mine. This guy was wearing a carbon copy of it.

"Let me hazard a guess," he said. "He's never told you he had a son."

CHAPTER SEVEN

I shook my head, and he laughed. Same laugh, even.

"I oughtn't be surprised. That sounds about like the old scalawag."

I didn't say anything for a few moments. I was trying to shake off the feeling that I'd been deep underwater and was just getting my head above the surface.

"I uh—I guess it just never came up," I said at last. "How did you know about his, um, that he was here?"

"I got a telegram. Uncle Gerald."

That took me a second to work out, too. I wasn't accustomed to hearing anyone use Pooter's official name.

He seemed to understand my discombobulation. "Can I buy you a cup of coffee?" He patted Dusty's shoulder. "The doctors say Pa's not likely to wake up for a while yet."

* * *

The cafeteria was just down the hallway. It was nearly deserted. Walt bought two coffees from a bored candy striper, and we sat at a scuffed and stained table in the corner.

"So Pa's never even mentioned to you that he was married?"

I tried not to choke on my first sip. "He's *married*?" You think you know a guy...

"*Was*," Walt said. "My ma's been gone some twenty years now."

"Sorry to hear it. That's tough on a kid." He gave me a close look, and I added. "I lost my mother when I was young, too."

"How old?"

"Fifteen."

He nodded. "I was twelve. It is hard, especially when..." He took a sip of coffee. "What about your father?"

"Died a couple years ago."

He made a sympathetic sound. "Were you close? I mean, after your mother passed on?"

"We were. For a while."

"And then?"

I lit a cigarette. Normally I didn't care to talk much about it. "We had a falling out not long before he died. Pretty much parted ways."

"I can sympathize."

"You and Dusty?"

He nodded. "Not a falling out, per se. More of a falling *away*. There's never been a quarrel between us or anything, but…" He paused to try his coffee. "He was always off chasing the rodeos when I was a boy, so we'd never really gotten to know each other all that much. Then Ma passed away, so we didn't even have that connection anymore. I lived with my grandparents while he was on the road, and when he *was* around, we just seemed to find less and less to say to each other."

He fished out a tortoise shell case, plucked a cigarette from it and lit it. "Then I finished school, went off to college and on to law school, and he came out here to be in pictures. We haven't seen each other since—just a letter once in a while. *How are you getting on?*—that sort of thing. Not that I blame him, really. It's no more his fault than mine."

"You do know it wasn't really all about the rodeos, or the movies, right?"

"Oh, yeah," He blew smoke at the ceiling. "He was bent on tracking down some owl hoot from his wild old lawman days. The one that got away. Though I doubt he ever caught up with him."

"As a matter of fact…" I ran down the story of how I'd first met Dusty and how we'd found his long-lost fugitive.

He stared for a moment when I'd finished. "Well, I *will* be damned. He never wrote me any of that."

I tapped my smoke in the ashtray. "So," I said, looking for a change of subject, "Do you live out here, or in Texas?"

"Arizona, actually."

"What are your plans? Will you be sticking around town for a while?"

"I will. At least until I see if he's—until we're out of the woods. What about you?"

"Me? Am I sticking around?"

"I mean, you being an investigator… Are you looking for who did this?"

CHAPTER SEVEN

"Officially, no. The cops in our fair city don't take too kindly to private involvement. Especially mine."

"Weren't you one of them once?"

"Yeah, once." I could see that wasn't answer enough. "That, pal, is a story for another time."

"Fair enough. But *unofficially?*"

"Unofficially, I'm going to do as much as I can get away with. And if I find the son of a bitch before the police do…" I thought about Rust's words to Jones. I just might find myself in a killing way.

I left Walt in Dusty's room. Before I went, I gave him one of my cards and wrote down his hotel and room number, and we agreed to keep one another informed. Meanwhile, I drove over to the Buscadero to see if Pooter had the place back in shape, and to find out for myself whether he had any clues on the break-in.

"Howdy, Nate." It was the first time I'd ever come in that he hadn't greeted me with his knuckle-busting handshake and a hearty, "Pooter there, pard!" I felt for the guy—he was taking Dusty's shooting pretty hard.

The bar appeared to be back to normal, but it wasn't too busy. There were three or four young cowboys, nobody I knew, sitting brooding at a table, plus one wizened old-timer who sat near the far end of the bar, half asleep over his whiskey.

I told Pooter about meeting Walt, and he said he'd given his godson—Walt hadn't mentioned that—my name and number and assured him I would be on the job. I wished I had as much confidence. Word had already gotten around about Rust's murder, and Pooter filled me in on some wild cowboy theories about it. He said that things were more tense than ever between the divided groups. Queenan was evidently sitting on the fact that they were looking for Chipman, so Rust's pals were now suspicious of every cowboy who'd taken the Jones side, thinking he might be the one who'd slipped in the knife.

I didn't mention names or particulars but didn't see any harm in letting Pooter know the cops already had a suspect and that Rust's killing didn't appear to have any connection to Jones. *At least not to his shooting*, I thought, but I kept that part to myself. I hoped letting him know that much might keep things from getting out of hand. Anyway, it was just a matter of time before Chipman was run to ground, whether by the police or—with any luck at all—by me.

Chapter Eight

Doc Reese was humming a cheerful tune when I walked in. He was engrossed in his work and didn't see me. He was leaning over the body on his steel worktable, its chest fileted open and the shiny organs exposed. He was just inserting a rib spreader, and I watched, impressed at the strength the doc—who was close to eighty—still had in his thin forearms. He bore down on the handles of the spreader, and with a sharp crack, the rib cage opened like a clam shell.

"Sounds like Babe Ruth planting one into deep center field," I said.

He didn't flinch at all. The things Doc had seen in his forty years on the job, there was no startling the old man. He just turned half around and looked me up and down through his thick lenses.

"Nate Ross, bearing gifts." He stood upright, laid the spreader on a tray, and peeled off his rubber gloves. He pointed at the box in my hand. "Something tells me it's business that brings you into my inner sanctum."

"There's no fooling you, Doc."

I set the box on the nearby desk. It held twenty El Wadoras, probably the worst cigars ever produced. For reasons I couldn't understand, they were Doc's favorites. In his line, maybe he'd developed a fondness for foul smells. In any case, they were the usual fee I paid for a favor from the old deputy coroner.

Before I could state the object of my visit, Doc made a sympathetic face. "I heard your associate, the cowboy fellow, was shot."

"Dusty Vanner, yeah."

"Seriously hurt?"

"Serious enough, I guess. Surgery went okay, though, so it doesn't look like he'll be coming your way anytime soon. Although if I have my way, someone else might be."

He smiled. "On the warpath, as usual. Is that why you're here?"

"No, I'm working something else at the moment. It's to do with Ty Jones."

"Ah, yes, the Great Hollywood Shootout." He gave me a wink. "So I take it if Queenan or his boys come around, we never had this talk?"

"Don't worry about that. It's not the shooting I'm working on. In fact, that case is probably dead in the water now, so to speak." I told him about Rust's killing, which he hadn't gotten the word on yet.

"All I'm after right now is a look at Ty Jones's personal effects, if they're still here."

"They're here," Doc said. "Nobody's come forward to claim the body yet." He gave me a searching look. "His belongings certainly seem to be popular, though."

"What do you mean?"

"A young woman came in a few days back claiming to be his wife. She wanted to pick up his things. We had him on record as unmarried, so I told her I couldn't release anything without a court order."

Unless I missed my guess, the "wife" was Hazel Rust. She wasn't missing a trick in looking for clues to where Jones might have stashed the painting.

"Then, the day before yesterday," Doc went on, "A 'brother' turned up with the same request. I'd had no word from the police about any next of kin, so I referred him to the court as well."

I took the mug shot out of my pocket and showed it to Doc. "Any chance this is the brother?"

He adjusted his glasses on his nose and peered at the photo. "Yes, I'd say that was him."

"Did you let either one of these people look through Jones's stuff?"

"Of course not. Although the brother was so adamant, I did open the box and show him what was inside."

"Did he say anything about it?"

"No, but he seemed bothered, as though it wasn't what he expected to see."

CHAPTER EIGHT

"Okay if I have a look at the stuff?"

"I suppose so." He picked up the box from the desk, gave it an appreciative sniff, and dropped it into a drawer. *"Your* papers seem to be in order."

He went over to the back wall, where floor-to-ceiling shelves held rows of cardboard cartons with numbered tags attached. He mumbled to himself as he ran a finger down one row and stopped. "Ah, here we are."

He slid the box out and carried it over to the desk. As he lifted off the top, I could see it held mostly clothing, plus a light gray cowboy hat and a pair of fancy stitched boots. I went through everything, checked inside the lining of the hat and under the hatband, even pulled the insoles out of the boots and looking under them. Nothing.

I could tell the curiosity was getting to Doc. He's a guy who likes to know things. "Something in particular you're looking for? Gold coins? Diamonds, perhaps?"

"Would you believe a stolen painting?"

* * *

Hazel Rust had lied to me. Not *lied* so much as held out. It didn't surprise me—I listen to lies for a living and I figured I'd find out soon enough whether she was leading me down a garden path. Queenan and Grumman were more than willing to have me notify her about her husband's murder, and I welcomed the chance to give her that news before the cops did. I knew her reaction would likely tell me whether she'd also lied about her connection with Chipman, had been in cahoots with him all along, or maybe had just lately thrown in with him for a piece of the goods. With women like her, you could never be sure.

If she *had* told me the truth about Chipman, she might still be in danger. My guess was that Chipman had gone to Rust thinking he'd have a line on the painting. He had to have tossed the place before he killed Rust—I'd come on the scene too soon after. And killing Rust didn't make much sense if he'd gotten what he was looking for. If he was still hunting for it, he might think about taking another run at Hazel. So either way, I needed to pay her a visit.

I parked under the closest streetlight I could find to her hotel. It was that sort of neighborhood. She'd told me her room number was 313. But being the doubting Thomas that I am, I stopped at the desk and offered the mousy little clerk a five spot for a peek at the register. His sleepy blue eyes faked boredom, but I could tell they were cataloging me down to my tie pin in case he needed to describe me later. It was that sort of place.

He took the bill, anyway, and spun the register around for me. *Hazel Rust—313.* Good girl.

"No trouble now, Mister," the clerk said. I couldn't tell whether it was a question or a warning.

"Just visiting a sick friend," I said over my shoulder as I headed toward the elevator. The self-operating car didn't look any too serviceable, so I opted for the stairs. The moment the stairwell door shut behind me, I was washed in the stink of dust, mildew, stale cigarette smoke, rank sweat, and a hint of vomit. It made me wish I'd risked the elevator. The cockroaches didn't seem to mind it. I zigzagged around them, taking shallow breaths through my mouth as I made my way up the stairs, careful not to catch my toes in the rips of the carpeting.

I came through the door at the third-floor landing and took two or three gulps of what, by comparison, was as sweet as mountain air. I took a quick sniff at my suit and scraped the odd roach or two off my shoes before I started down the dingy hallway in search of room 313.

I was knocking for the third time when I saw a flicker of movement behind the peephole, and the door opened. Hazel looked at me without comment, then poked her head out and checked both ways down the hallway before she waved me in.

Overall, the room was better than I'd expected from what I had seen of the place. It wasn't a Biltmore suite, but it was reasonably clean. The furniture looked cheap but seemed in good repair, and the carpet had only a handful of cigarette burns.

Hazel was dressed for staying in, in a pair of baby blue pajamas under a dark blue velour robe. The robe's right-hand pocket sagged with the weight of what I assumed was her little .32 automatic. I didn't let it worry me.

CHAPTER EIGHT

"Have you found the painting?" That was all the greeting she gave me.

"Not yet." I took my hat off and sat on the sturdier looking of the two chairs I saw. I expected her to take the hint and sit in the other one. After a moment or two of indecision, she did.

"Have you found Pete, then?" She sounded hopeful, but I knew it could be an act.

"Not exactly. Listen, I'm afraid I have some bad news for you." She looked sincerely concerned. I didn't want to hit her with it too hard on the chance that she wasn't playing me for a sap. It was possible she wasn't in this scheme with Chipman, and it was even possible that she still cared at least a little about her husband. Still, there's never an easy way to deliver that kind of news. In the end, the best way is to come right out with it.

"Leo's dead." I said it as gently as I could, but studied her face as I did. I was primed for any sign of deception.

"Dead," she repeated in a toneless voice. "Dead, how?"

"Murdered," I said. "Stabbed in his apartment."

Her eyes went wide and stayed on mine for a few seconds, then slowly lowered to the floor between her slippered feet. A single tear fell between them, and her shoulders came up and sank again as she let out a heavy breath. I'd been prepared for a theatrical display of hysterics that would have told me she was playing me and already knew damn well her husband was dead. I'd also been prepared for a deadpan acceptance of the news. That wouldn't necessarily have meant she was involved in his death, only that she didn't care one way or the other. I was even ready for the normal reaction of a wife getting this news—disbelief, anger, weeping. But I was not expecting a silent show of sorrow that was as much guilt as grief.

"It's all my fault." She said it so softly I could barely make out the words. "If I'd never got mixed up in all of this. If I'd just stayed…" She looked up at me. "He wasn't always the best guy. He could be nasty when he was drinking, and he was pretty much always drinking." She shook her head. "But he didn't deserve that. Nobody does. What the hell have I done?" After a long silence, she spoke again. "How…how did you find out?"

"I went to talk to him. I found him not long after it happened." I took out the mug photo and held it out to her. "This guy was leaving just as I got there."

She stared at the photo, and her face went from dead pale to deep red. When she looked away and nodded, her eyes were black and bright with anger.

"Pete." She spat the name out like it was a bad taste she needed to be rid of. "I knew it." Her hand slid into her robe pocket, and I could tell she was gripping the little gun. "He must have thought Leo would know where it was. Poor Leo." She looked at me. "Are you going to find him?"

"I'm going to try," I said.

"When you do, I want you to kill him. Please?"

"First, I've got to find him. And maybe you can help with that. You didn't give me the whole story the other night. You forgot to mention that you'd been to the morgue to try and get Jones's things."

"I didn't think it mattered."

"Maybe it doesn't. But Chipman went there, too, claiming to be Jones's brother."

"Did he get Ty's things?"

"No, but they showed him what was in the box. It didn't make him happy. What did *you* expect to find?"

"I already told you. I thought maybe a claim check or something. A guy like him usually carries all his important stuff with him—paychecks, check stubs, parole papers—"

"Jones was on parole? You forgot to mention that, too."

She looked honestly surprised.

"I guess I just assumed you already knew that. He did time in the pen in Arizona. Not under Jones, under his real name."

"Which was...?"

"I don't know." She held up a defensive hand. "I swear I don't. He never would tell me."

"Why would it matter if he was on legit parole?"

"Because he had a case hanging over him here, from several years back. I don't know what, so don't ask. But Arizona wanted him—for murder, he

CHAPTER EIGHT

said." Again, she held up a hand. "I don't know the details. They shipped him out there, and he got ten years for manslaughter. They paroled him after five. Because he'd been extradited, California couldn't bring him back, he said. But he got to missing home, so he changed his name and came back here on his own. And he's been here ever since."

I could never understand smart, good-looking women falling for losers like Rust and Jones. But I figured it wouldn't get me any more cooperation from her if I pointed out her lousy taste in men, so I kept buttoned on the subject. I'd have to check on her story. I didn't really think she was lying now, but maybe Jones had lied to her. Ordinarily, I'd just ask Queenan to look into something like this, but I was already on thin ice with him where Jones and Rust were concerned. Plus, now that it seemed he was considering Jones's death a done deal, he wouldn't likely be interested in turning over any new rocks.

"Okay," I said. "Anything else you neglected to tell me about the guy? Anything that might help? Keep in mind, if I find the painting at this point, I'll probably find Chipman."

"I can't think of anything."

"You let me know if you do. I mean it." I stood up and put on my hat. "Meanwhile, you have someplace else you can go? Someplace where he's not likely to come knocking?"

She shook her head. "I'm not worried. He wouldn't have gone to Leo if he thought I could tell him anything else. I don't think he'll come around here." She took her hand with the .32 in it out of her pocket. "And if he does…".

"Yeah, well, keep your door double locked, just in case. I'll be in touch." She nodded and tucked the gun away again, and I went out and down the hall to the elevator.

* * *

I was happy to see that my car was still there and still in one piece. I sat behind the wheel and was thinking over all that Hazel had told me and trying to decide where I'd hide out if I were Pete Chipman when I noticed a guy stepping from the mouth of an alley about twenty feet ahead. He stopped in the shadow of the buildings like he was maybe going to light a smoke. I started the engine and turned on the headlights just as he brought the gun up.

In the flash of time before things started happening, I recognized Pete Chipman. He squinted in the light and shielded his eyes with one hand. With the other, he started pumping lead my way. My windshield blew out, and I heard the window next to my head shatter as I tromped my foot down on the gas and drove straight at him. Tiny chips of glass had gotten into my eyes, and suddenly, everything looked like I was seeing it through a kaleidoscope. I caught a vague image of Chipman ducking back into the alley just as my right front fender ground into the brick corner of a building, and I was slammed into the steering wheel.

The car jolted to a stop, and I half climbed, half fell out with my .380 in my hand, for what good it was going to do me. I listened to the sound of running feet retreating down the alley while I tried to get my breath and tried not to blink, hoping to keep from damaging my eyeballs or eyelids. From that same direction, I caught the sound of a motorcycle being kick-started and a roar as it sped away into the night.

Stumbling around, I heard a splash as I stepped into a pothole filled with water. I knew what the water would be like, but beggars can't be choosers. I knelt down and took up cupped handfuls, splashing the greasy liquid into my eyes again and again. After a couple of minutes of this, the puddle was nearly dry, and my vision was still a bit blurred, but good enough that I could navigate. Chipman, of course, was long gone, with nothing beyond the short alleyway to tell me which way he had headed.

My car was banged up but still drivable. I moved it back to where I'd parked it before, then hurried back into the hotel, hoping Chipman hadn't circled back and made his way there. The clerk stared hard at me when I came through the lobby, but he didn't ask.

Hazel answered my knock right away and gasped when she saw me. Between my red eyes, the glass still in my hair, and the grime all over my face from the filthy water, I must have been quite a sight.

CHAPTER EIGHT

I gave her a quick rundown and told her to pack her things while I used her bathroom to flush out my eyes with clean water and to make myself more or less presentable.

We went downstairs, and I left her in the lobby while I checked the street for any signs of a motorcycle, or Chipman. Satisfied, I pulled to the front of the hotel, loaded Hazel and her two suitcases up, and drove off.

I kept a close watch while we drove but didn't spot any motorbikes tailing us, so I'd relaxed a little by the time I reached the Rosslyn. I'd called ahead and made arrangements with Dickie to register "Jane Smith."

Dickie showed us to a twelfth-floor room. It was small and plain, but it sat smack in the middle of a long hallway. It had only one small window that looked out on a courtyard, and there was no fire escape there, so the only way to reach the room was by coming down the hallway. Dickie promised to keep it monitored.

"What are the odds this bird's going to come skulking around?" Dickie asked me, as we took the elevator down after getting Hazel settled.

"I don't think it's likely," I told him. "I'm sure we weren't followed, and I doubt he'd think to look for her here. Anyway, it sounds as if he'd already been here and gone through Jones's room before she did, so for all he knows, the word's out, and he'll be watched for. But just in case..." I pulled out Chipman's mug and handed it to him. "There's your boy."

He studied it and started to pass it back, but I held up a hand. "Keep it."

"You ain't going to need it?"

"No, I've already seen that face more times than I care to. I'll know it if I see it again."

Chapter Nine

The face that greeted me in the mirror the next morning was none too pretty. My aching eyes were Skid Row red, and I had dried blood caked on in two or three spots from small cuts and scratches. I knew I should probably have a doctor look me over before I did anything else, but my eyes seemed to be working just fine, and I had other things to do.

After I showered, shaved, and breakfasted, I loaded Monte into the car. It seemed to me that up until then, I'd been in a race with Pete Chipman to find Hart's painting. I was tired of the guy showing up and getting in my way, and I was definitely tired of him shooting at me. It was more personal now. It was time for me to do the showing up and to take him out of the picture one way or another.

Before I could go on the hunt, I needed to line up some transportation. Driving around with half of my windows shot out wasn't going to fly for long, but the repair shop I used was closed until eight, so I drove over to the Buscadero first. The wind that whistled through between the busted-out windshield and side window stung my sore eyeballs and kept trying to snatch my hat off. After the third time I had to readjust it, I took the damn thing off and tossed it on the floor. Monte seemed to enjoy the steady breeze—he sat up straight with his eyes closed, tongue hanging out, and a sunny smile on his face.

"Howdy, Nate," Pooter said as we came in. Again, not his normal salutation—he was clearly still down in the dumps. He had just opened the doors and was taking upended chairs off the tables when he noticed my

CHAPTER NINE

face. "Good God, you look like hell! You all right?"

"Just enjoying a little L.A. nightlife."

I could tell he was dying to ask, but he let it ride. He brightened a little when Monte trotted over to have his ears scratched. "Hey there, you big rascal. Come to keep old Pooter company today?"

"No, I'm taking him along with me today." That seemed to bring Pooter down again, so I made a quick change of subject. "Have you been to see Dusty yet?"

He ruffled the big dog's fur and looked up. "Yeah, I closed up early last night and went by. Walt said he stirred a bit in his sleep."

"That's a good sign, I guess. I'm going to go by later and see how he is." I looked around the room. "Looks like you got everything back in order."

"Yep. It looked worse than it was. A lot of glassware busted up, but only a few bottles broke." He pushed a finger under his hatband and scratched his head. "I still can't see what they was after. Didn't take so much as a pint of whiskey. The police find out anything yet?"

"Last I heard, they're as stumped as we are." I didn't tell him what Queenan had said about Dusty's gun, or the fingerprints. I decided to go ahead and tell him about Pete Chipman killing Rust—he'd hear about it soon enough anyway. Western Union has nothing on the cowboy grapevine.

His eyes went wide at the news. "Damn, poor old Rust. I never liked the fella, but..." He sat down in one of the chairs.

"Do you know Chipman?"

"Yeah, I know him. Not well. He's not a friendly fellow—kind of a standoffish sort. We've worked a few of the same jobs, and he's come in here plenty, of course." He took his hat off and laid it on the table and looked up at me. "But why the hell would he want to kill Leo Rust?"

I told him about Hart's painting and the racket Chipman and Jones had been running. He promised me he'd keep that part to himself.

He whistled. "I'll be damned. I never figured Ty Jones for that type. The last Charlie Russell, you say? I expect that would be worth a good bit of change." He snorted. "A whole lot more than mine, anyhow."

"What do you mean *yours*?"

He pointed to the framed picture behind the bar, of the cowboys riding into the hotel.

"That's a Russell?"

He looked at me with something like pity. "It is. My ma sent it to me when we opened this place. It used to hang in my pa's study back home. Just a print, of course. Hell, the frame probably cost more than the picture."

He stood and walked over to where the print hung. "It's signed on the back, though. Pa had met ol' Charlie once when I was just a young buck. Here, I'll show you." He lifted the big frame off the wall with both hands and laid it face down on the bar. He dug out a pocketknife and had just opened it when he took a closer look at the back of the frame.

"Well, now, that's peculiar."

"What?"

"There's supposed to be nails in the back to hold the picture in." He pointed with the blade. "But they're gone, every damn one of them. Like somebody's pulled them out."

I stepped over and could see small holes around the frame's inner edge where the nails had been. I didn't think much about it at first, but then it hit me.

"Don't touch it," I told him. "I need to call the police."

* * *

Monte sat up and growled as my office door banged open.

"I gotta hand it to you, Ross. That was some hunch you had." Queenan breezed in with an ape smile on his face. "What's that they say about stopped clocks?"

He never got tired of giving me the razoo, but at the moment, I was happy to let it ride. I had a hunch why he was there.

He plopped down in a guest chair, and Monte turned up the growl. He'd never been fond of Queenan. Maybe his taste in associates was better than mine.

"Call your pet wolf off, will you?"

CHAPTER NINE

"*Monte.*" He read my tone and flopped back down with a huff, his eyes tight on Queenan.

"The prints matched?" I asked.

"Just got off the line with Ray Pinker. He did the comparisons himself. Vanner's gun, the Jones casing, the picture from the hootenanny bar—all the same bird."

"Still no i.d. on them?"

He threw his hands up. "We ain't miracle workers. If the guy's not in the files, he's not in the files."

"Okay. So where do we stand now?"

He squinted one eye and peered at me through his cigar fog. "There you go again with the *we* stuff. You got a mouse in your pocket, or what?"

"Come on, Cap. Your cases and mine have to be connected. Look, what I'm trying to find is a stolen painting, all right? And one of the guys who stole it." I thought I'd better loosen up and at least let him know what I was after, though I still planned to keep Hart's name to myself. "Don't you think odds are that a painting might be what whoever shot Dusty was after? Why else take the back off that print? It'd be a perfect place to hide a stolen canvas."

"But you're telling me this Chipman turd is your guy? There ain't nothing to show he was in that bar, other than maybe as a customer. We have his prints, remember?"

"So maybe he's got another partner."

"Like who? Vanner's partner, Barnes?"

"Of course not. I don't know who. But he was supposed to have had a buyer already lined up for the painting. Maybe with Jones out of the picture the two of them have thrown in together."

"If it's the buyer who broke into the bar, I can see him shootin' Vanner—he got caught dirty—but why set Rust up to shoot Jones?"

"I don't know, Cap. I admit it doesn't seem to make sense. But I also know you don't believe in coincidences any more than I do."

He considered that. "I ain't gonna say I agree with you. But connected or not, I guess the best shot for both of us at making some headway is to find Chipman."

"I'm working on that, soon as I can get on the road."

"Yeah, speakin' of that, I was going to ask." He angled his big chin toward the window that looked out on the gravel parking lot. "What the hell happened to your bucket? And your mug, for that matter? You been letting Rin Tin Tin here drive?"

"I had a little accident last night."

He gave me the cop's eye. "Uh-huh. That 'little accident' seems to have put a couple bullet holes through your windows." He waited for an answer, and I figured I could either shoot him, sic Monte on him, or tell him. I picked the peaceful route, or so I thought.

"Jesus, Ross!" I'd seen his face turn a dozen different shades of red before, but I'd never seen it go purple. Even Monte backed away a little. "You lost what little brains you had? We've talked about this kind of shit. You know, we could solve a crime in this burg once in a while if numbskulls like you would report this type of thing. We coulda maybe put the bite on this guy last night, but thanks to you, he's still runnin' around out there. You been palling around with these damn cowboys so long you're starting to behave like one of 'em."

He stabbed a finger at me. "Well, get this. There ain't but one Tom Mix in this world, and you ain't him." He stood and leaned over the desk toward me. "So you banged your fender on a brick wall, huh? I swear, I got half a mind to run you in for hit and run."

I just sat back and let his temper run its course. I knew it would. I also knew he had a point, not that I was about to admit that to him. He sat back down, and after a couple of minutes of muttered curses and heavy breathing, his eyes stopped bugging out and his normal color came back. He trimmed and lit a cigar and took a few thoughtful puffs before he spoke again.

"We're gonna make a deal right now, you and me. I want this asshole Chipman for the Rust kill. On the wild chance you're right, maybe we'll tag him for bein' in on the Vanner thing, too. Shootin' at you, I'm inclined to give him a break on—right now, I'm considerin' that more or less a public service. Point is, I want him. If you want him too, okay. But no more cowboying. You run across this guy, or you find out where he is, you let me know. And I

CHAPTER NINE

mean p.d.q., not after you've pulled some fresh dumb ass stunt." He fixed me with a fierce gaze. "We're agreed on that." It wasn't a question.

"Okay, Cap." There wasn't much else I could say.

"Okay, then." He stood again and put his hat on, gave me one final, disgusted look, and turned for the door. On his way out, he stopped and looked down at Monte. "You keep your boss out of trouble now, you hear me, boy?"

Instead of growling, Monte looked up and gave a nervous thump of his tail. Queenan walked out, and I could hear him mumbling to himself all the way down the hall.

Monte ambled over and laid his big head on my knee. I ran my hand over it, and he wagged his tail.

"A lot of help you were," I said. "Coward."

Chapter Ten

Half an hour after Queenan left, my pal Arnie showed up from his repair shop to pick up my damaged car and to leave off the vehicle he'd agreed to loan me. I wasn't expecting much, and Arnie didn't disappoint. I walked around the eyesore he'd brought me—a battered pickup, six or seven years old—and took in the details. Cracked windshield, bald, mismatched tires, body that had started off as sky blue but was now five different colors—six if you counted the rust. The tattered seat had once been beige but was coated with so much grease and accumulated grime that it had turned a dark tobacco brown.

I guess Arnie could read my face. He looked insulted. "Unless you want to borrow a tow truck, it's all I got, Nate. Take it or leave it." He held out the keys.

"It'll be fine, Arnie. I appreciate the loan." I hoped I sounded more sincere than I felt. I took the keys.

Arnie whistled as he looked over the damage to my car, "Say, didn't I replace that side window just a few months ago?"

"That was on my old crate. I just bought this one recently."

He ran his hand over the crumpled fender, the crooked bumper, and the bent grille. "Well, I see you're getting 'er nice and broke in."

"So, when do I get it back? Tomorrow? The day after?"

Arnie winced. "If it was just the bodywork and the one window, I could maybe swing it. But nobody local has a windshield to fit. Closest one I could find is in Fresno, and they won't even put it on the truck until day after tomorrow. Means you're looking at five days, easy."

CHAPTER TEN

I didn't want to offend the guy any more than I had, so kept my complaint to myself. But I couldn't help casting a gloomy eye over my temporary transportation. Even Monte seemed dissatisfied with the arrangement. He looked at me, at the decrepit heap, then at me again as if to say, "*You* can ride in that thing, pal, but count me out."

I handed Arnie my keys, and he drove off. I took a closer look inside the truck. It didn't improve my impression of it any. Arnie hadn't even bothered to dust out the cobwebs. While I closed and locked it—as though I had to worry about anybody stealing it—Monte sniffed at a front tire, hiked his leg, and turned loose a stream.

"Buddy," I said. "I couldn't agree more."

I left Monte in the office while I took Arnie's truck for a test drive. The clutch was loose and sloppy, and the tappets clacked like maracas, but it seemed to have power enough. I could tolerate it for a few days. It was a quick test—I only drove as far as Queen of Angels to check and see how Dusty was getting on. And to ask for some assistance with my case.

Walt was sitting in a chair next to Dusty's bed when I walked in. He was looking pretty ragged, and despite the change of clothes I was guessing he hadn't been away for long and probably hadn't gotten any sleep. Dusty was still sleeping, and maybe it was wishful thinking, but he looked better than he had before. His color was a lot better, and his breathing was quieter and more rhythmic.

"How's he doing?" I asked, trying to keep my voice low.

"Better. He was actually awake for a little while an hour or so ago." He gave me a tired smile. "He was asking for you."

"Yeah? He say anything about what happened?"

He shook his head. "Just rambled. Nothing that made sense. He talked like he was on a movie shoot. It was only for two or three minutes, then he went back to sleep, and he's been out ever since."

"Have the cops been here?"

"Yes. A couple of detectives, Valverde and Deacon, were here to see if they could get a statement. He wasn't awake yet then. They said they'd try later."

"I can hold the fort here for a while if you want to go get a couple hours' sleep. You look about done in."

"No, I'll be fine. But thanks."

"Okay. I've got some stuff to do, then, but I'll stop by again later. Meanwhile, call me if he wakes up, will you? I need to know whatever he can tell us."

He said he would, and I turned to go. I stopped in the doorway. I'd almost forgotten my other reason for coming. "Say, do you have any contacts with the state prison in Arizona?"

He swiveled in his chair to look at me. "Is it something to do with Pa's shooting?"

"No, I've gotten all I can about that from the police for now. There's not much more I can do until I can talk to Dusty. This is about the other thing I've been working on."

"Well, I used to sit on a committee with the assistant warden at Florence. We played a few rounds of golf now and then."

"Would you be able to get a prison record out of him?"

"I'd imagine so. Whose?"

"There's the tricky part—I don't know. The guy I'm interested in did his time under a different name than the one I have."

"How would he know who to look for, then?"

"I've got a pal on the newspaper who could wire him a photo. Fingerprints, too, if I can get my hands on them."

"Well, I'll be happy to make a call if it helps."

"I appreciate it."

* * *

I drove to the office and made two calls, the first one to Doc Reese. For a box of El Wadoras on account, he said he'd furnish me with a photostat copy of Ty Jones's fingerprint card. Next, I called Aggie Underwood at the *Herald-Express*. Normally, I'd have to stand the gaff from her if I asked for a

CHAPTER TEN

favor—she couldn't resist giving me a hard time. But I'd fed her some inside dope on a gambling joint roust just the month before, and she'd bagged a front-page story out of it. So, at the moment, I occupied the catbird's seat.

I still had to remind her of that, but after some token grumbling, she said she'd pull a photo of Jones from the paper's files, and she agreed to wire it and Jones's prints once I had them, to Walt's golf buddy in Arizona.

Next, I called the Rosslyn to check with Dickie. Hazel was fine and there'd been no sign of Pete Chipman. I couldn't do much more until I got the Jones items. It had been a busy morning, and I hadn't eaten much. Monte had started snoozing beside the desk while I was on the line with Dickie. He made a grumbling noise when I nudged him awake.

"Come on, *chico*. Lunchtime." He got to his feet, shot me a baleful look, and followed me out, but he perked up plenty when he saw where we were going.

* * *

When we went back upstairs afterward, I could hear the phone ringing before I reached my door. I got the door unlocked and answered on the fourth ring.

"Nate, it's Walt."

"Everything okay?"

"Fine—Pa's still out, but things look good. I just wanted to let you know I got in touch with George Walcott at the prison in Florence. He says if you send him the photograph and fingerprints, he'll see what he can find."

"All right, good. Thanks for lining that up—it'll be a big help. I owe you one."

"You don't, but on that topic, I was going to ask a favor."

"Name it."

"I'm starting to go stir-crazy sitting around this place. A man can only do so many crossword puzzles. I thought about going over to spend some time with Uncle Gerald, but sitting in a bar all day long isn't any more appealing. I started thinking after you left… I wondered if you'd let me tag along with you for a while."

"Tag along?"

"I'm feeling pretty useless here, and if some of what you're doing is looking into who shot Pa, I'd really like to be part of that, to help if I can." He paused. "Sorry, maybe I shouldn't have asked."

"No, there's no need to apologize. You just caught me by surprise, that's all. I've never had anybody ask that before. It's okay with me, I guess. But I'll warn you, it's nothing like the pulp magazines. Most of what I do day to day isn't all that exciting."

He laughed. "You want to talk unexciting? I started out as a probate lawyer. Anyway, it could hardly be less interesting than warming a chair in a hospital room watching a man sleep."

"Yeah, we'll see if you still think that after a couple hours of gumshoeing. I was just leaving the office—I could be there in ten minutes if you're ready."

"Trust me, I'm more than ready."

* * *

I poked my head back in at Gus's, and before I could even ask, Benjy came over to collect Monte.

"Leave him as long as you need to, boss," he said. As Benjy walked toward the office with Monte following, I heard him say, "You look hungry, boy." Maybe leaving him in a diner with a soft touch like Benjy was a bad idea.

* * *

Dusty was still out, so I didn't spend much time at the hospital. Walt told the nurse he'd be back later, and we walked out to where I'd parked Arnie's truck. I guess Walt was too polite to say anything, but the look on his face said plenty.

"It's a loan from my mechanic. He's got my car for a few days. If you want to change your mind—"

He grinned. "Not at all. It looks…serviceable."

"I guess we'll see. My office is less than a mile away, so this is as far as I've driven it yet."

CHAPTER TEN

I jackrabbited a little as I pulled out onto Vermont. "Sorry," I said. "Haven't got the feel of this jalopy yet."

"What's your car in the garage for?"

"A little body work and some new glass."

"Glass?"

"Windshield and front driver's side window."

He gave me a curious look. "What happened?"

"I had a little misadventure last night."

"What sort of misadventure breaks windows?"

"Geez, you lawyers are worse than cops. Nothing but questions. A guy shot at me." His look went from curious to horrified, so I added, "He missed."

"So much for your lack of excitement."

"Oh, no. A rare exception. Lucky for me."

"Was this anything to do with what happened to Pa?" I looked over at the question, and he raised his hands. "Sorry, force of habit."

I wasn't usually keen on sharing much information, but I figured he had the right to know. "I'm not sure yet, but it's possible."

"Is that what we're doing? Looking for this man?"

"*We* are going to pick up fingerprints for your friend at the prison, then over to see my pal at the newspaper."

"Is *that* related to Pa's shooting?"

"It is, and it isn't." I wasn't looking at him, but I could feel the question. "I'm not trying to play the cloak-and-dagger game on you here. The guy who did time in the Arizona pokey is dead. Before he died, he stole a painting and hid it. His cohort's trying to find it, and I'm trying to get to it first. The partner is the guy who tried to shoot me."

"I don't see the connection to Pa."

"I'm getting to that. It's looking like whoever shot Dusty may have had a hand in killing the first guy."

"The one who took the painting."

"Right. And that guy's partner's in the clear on the shootings so far. But it also looks like the painting is what Dusty's shooter was after."

"So the partner may have competition?"

"That, or he's found a new partner."

"What would make them think this painting would be at Pa's saloon?"

"I'm not sure, except that these guys—the ones I know about anyway—are all movie cowboys, and all do their drinking at the Buscadero. And the painting's by a cowboy artist named Charles Russell."

"Charlie Russell?"

"You know him?"

"Well, *of* him. You don't grow up in Texas and not know who Charlie Russell was. Is it one of his earlier works?"

"Actually, it's his *final* work."

"Good Lord. That would be worth a fortune!"

"Bingo."

Chapter Eleven

Our first visit was to Doc Reese to pick up a copy of Jones's fingerprints. Walt insisted on going in with me, never mind my warning. You can always tell a lawyer, but you can't tell him much. It was clear right away that he regretted not listening to me. Doc has a way with visitors—especially first-timers. He had a not-so-fresh one open on the table and we had to stand and wait while he examined stomach contents.

Between the gutted body, Doc's detailed, running commentary on what he found in the stomach, and the sight and smell of the half-eaten Reuben sandwich sitting on Doc's desk, Walt's face was the color of a five-dollar bill by the time we left. The devil in me entertained the thought of suggesting we grab something to eat before our next stop, but Arnie's truck already smelled bad enough without adding Walt's own stomach contents to the mix.

"Our next stop should be a little easier on the senses," I promised as Walt started to get his color back. "Unless the smell of printer's ink gets to you."

* * *

Aggie Underwood was on the phone when we walked into the busy city room. She was holding a heated discussion with whoever was on the other end. Even over the buzz of other conversations, the clack of a dozen typewriters, and the bustle of copyboys tripping over each other in their rush to carry fresh pages to the editor's office, her voice carried.

"It'll be in the evening edition with or without your side of the story," she was saying into the mouthpiece. "And don't think for one second it's going to say you were 'unavailable for comment.' 'Refused comment' is how it'll read." There was a pause while she listened and rolled her eyes. "Okay, fine. You call me back when you decide. But remember I'm on a deadline. Always a pleasure, councilman."

She plunked the receiver down, not quite hard enough to crack it, and looked up at me. "God, I hate politicians."

"Doesn't everybody?"

I introduced Walt to her, and her tone changed in a flash. She simpered at him like a schoolgirl when he offered his hand.

"It's wonderful to finally meet you, Walter," she said in a more genteel voice than I'd ever heard her use with me or anyone else. "How's your poor father doing?"

"Holding his own, thank you, ma'am."

"I'm glad to hear it. Such a fine man. He's told me so much about you."

"He *has*?" I didn't mean it to sound quite so indignant. "He's never said diddly-do to me."

Aggie cocked an eyebrow. "Have you ever asked?"

"Well, no. Never thought about it, I guess."

"Oh, you *men*." She rolled her eyes again and made an exasperated sound. Now *there* was the Aggie I knew. She folded her hands on the desk. "Anyway, I guess you're here to bring me some prints."

I held up the card Doc had given me. Aggie rooted around in a tray on her desk and came out with a photograph. It was a head-and-shoulders shot of Jones in his cowboy getup. It was the same one I'd seen in the paper—one of those studio photos the casting agents used.

"I hope this'll work for you. We only have a couple of others of him in the files, but they're group shots, and he's wearing the hat in all of them."

"The face is plenty clear—it should do." I handed it back, along with the prints. "The guy you need to wire them to is George…" I looked at Walt.

"Walcott."

"Right, George Walcott. How soon can you send them off?"

Aggie winked at Walt. "Always in a hurry, this guy." She turned to me. "Right now, I've got to wait for a call back from that chickensh—" She glanced

CHAPTER ELEVEN

at Walt. *"Lily-livered* councilman." She checked her watch. "Give me an hour and a half. Less, if there's nothing going out on the wire ahead of me."

"I owe you one, Ag."

"And don't you forget it. You can bet *I* won't." She looked at Walt and turned on the charm again. "Walter, I hope you won't let this one get you into any trouble. Trouble is what he does best."

Walt promised to be careful, and to pass on her regards to Dusty, and said how delighted he was to meet her, and so on, while Aggie listened to his smooth Texas accent with stars in her eyes. We took our leave, and I hustled Walt out of there before Aggie forgot she was a married woman.

"Charming lady," Walt remarked as we climbed back into Arnie's junk pile.

I nodded. "Yeah, she's a peach. Cut your throat for a story, but she's still a peach."

"Where to now?"

"Someplace where a guy from Texas ought to feel right at home."

* * *

It took a lot to turn heads—the locals' heads anyways—in Hollywood, but Arnie's truck drew some curious looks as we rattled down Sunset. I managed to find parking right on the boulevard, half a block from Gower. I'd explained to Walt along the way that this was the daytime gathering spot for all the film cowboys who spent their evenings at Dusty and Pooter's bar. Mornings were best to catch a crowd here, but even as late in the day as it was, there was a fair number of the boys around. Small knots of them stood here and there on the sidewalk, joshing and telling tall stories. I knew there'd be plenty more inside the drug store, either at the lunch counter or lurking around the payphone, hoping to land a late call out or line up work for the next day.

I was looking to get a line on Pete Chipman's whereabouts. Hazel had said he'd roomed here and there with a couple of the cowboys, though she didn't know who. I was hoping I might turn up somebody who could point me the right way. The trick was getting them to talk. These cowboys were a fiercely private bunch and lived by the code that a man's business was his own. They could be gossipy as hell within their own ranks, but with outsiders there was a wall of silence that was tough to breach.

Thanks to Dusty, and a couple of past cases, I was in fairly good standing with many of the cowboys. Not a member of the club, but not a total outsider either. And now that I had a genuine Texan—Dusty Vanner's son, no less—riding shotgun, I felt pretty certain I might get some answers. I'd have to watch my step—the Rust/Jones mess was still an open sore, and I could assume that Chipman belonged in the Jones camp. Also, I had no way of knowing if word had already spread to them that the cops wanted Chipman for killing Rust.

I started with a couple of the men I knew a little, and they shook their heads and passed me off to a couple of others. This went on through four or five rounds, and I was getting nowhere. I didn't come up against any open hostility, and none of them seemed evasive or even reluctant. But after a couple of hours, when Walt and I had each quizzed every cowboy we could find, and none of them claimed to know where we might find Chipman, I decided we should move along.

Gower Gulch being a bust, I pointed us back towards the office. We ducked into Gus's first to eat some dinner. It might have been my imagination, but I thought Monte looked heavier than when I'd left him. The big mutt took an instant liking to Walt, helped along by the T-bone scraps Walt fed him from his plate. We talked strategy and agreed we'd try our luck with the cowboys at the Buscadero later. Many of them would be guys who'd been out on jobs earlier, so we'd have a different group to question. And alcohol would make them a little more talky.

* * *

The Buscadero wasn't nearly as busy as I expected it to be. Pooter told us that one of the bigger studios had siphoned off a lot of the day players for a major shoot out near Lone Pine, and it was expected to go for a couple of days. Aside from only a handful of different faces, the crowd mainly consisted of cowpokes Walt and I had already questioned. And none of the newcomers

CHAPTER ELEVEN

were any more help. The Rust crowd didn't know where Chipman might be and if the Jones bunch did, they weren't saying.

After talking to everyone we could, Walt and I spent another hour nursing beers and making meaningless small talk with Pooter and a couple of the cowboys. Then we decided to call it a night and try another plan of attack in the morning. I dropped Walt off at the hospital, went back to the diner to collect my furry roommate, and headed home.

Chapter Twelve

I'd slept a little later than I'd planned. Maybe the last couple of days were catching up with me. I drove with Monte to the office and was planning to leave him there while I went to the hospital to check on Dusty and pick up Walt. I was taking a quick look through the morning mail first when the bell over my door sounded, and Walt walked in. He was a little winded, and my first thought was Dusty.

I stood up. "Everything okay?" I asked him, hoping I didn't sound overanxious.

He held up a hand. "He's fine. No change. I just got some news back from Arizona that I thought I better pass on right away." I dropped back into my chair, and he took a seat.

"You could have just called."

"It's all right. I needed a little fresh air and exercise."

"I take it your pal at the prison came through, then?"

"He did. He didn't even need the prints—the photograph was plenty. He recognized Jones right off." He took out a pocket notebook, flipped through a couple of pages.

"His true name was Tirone Bianco. Arizona extradited him from California in late 1932 to stand trial for murder. He and a partner had been in the act of burglarizing a saddle shop in Prescott the year before when the owner surprised them and threw down on them with a shotgun. There was a struggle over the gun, and it discharged—accidentally, according to the burglars—and the owner was killed. Both men ended up pleading guilty to manslaughter, and instead of a possible life term, they each received a ten-year sentence.

CHAPTER TWELVE

Jones—or Bianco—was released after five."

"You say he was extradited from here. Hazel told me he claimed he still had something over his head in California. Any idea what?"

Walt shook his head. "George didn't have anything on that. All that's in the file is the extradition order. But I suppose it explains the alias." He laughed. "The fool would have been wiser to stay in Arizona, where he'd be safe."

"What do you mean?"

"Having been extradited—essentially taken against his will—out of state, he couldn't legally be forced to return to California. But if he came back on his own..."

"I'll be damned. Nobody ever said crooks were smart. How about the partner—what was his story?"

His face broke out in a Cheshire Cat grin. "Oh, I was hoping you'd ask me that. The partner died at Florence four years ago of typhus."

I couldn't see anything too astounding in that. "And...?"

"His name was Chipman. *Peter* Chipman."

* * *

For once, I was happy to keep a promise to Queenan. He'd told me to let him know if and when I found Pete Chipman. Well, it looked like I'd found him, but instead of answering all of our questions, it only brought up new ones. If Pete Chipman was dead, who was this bird shooting and stabbing his way across L.A., claiming to be him? It turned into even more of a head-scratcher when Walt's buddy Walcott wired Peter Chipman's prison file to Queenan, complete with fingerprints and mugshot. The photo was our boy, all right, but the prints didn't match the ones in L.A.P.D.'s files.

I'd left Walt back at the hospital with Dusty. I figured Doc Reese was enough—I thought I should spare him Queenan, at least for the time being. Since I'd brought this straight to Queenan, he was playing nice for once and let me have a peek at the prison file while we sat in his office. I looked through the summary of the case that had sent Chipman there. It listed Bianco and described the crime that had landed them both in Florence. I couldn't find anything in there, or elsewhere, that was helpful—nothing we didn't know about already—until I got to a section that listed known associates and family members.

I looked up at Queenan. "Hey, Cap, didn't you tell me this guy and his brother were pinched on some sort of burglary rap back in the day?"

"Yeah, in '32, if I recall. All's they got was a short dip in county jail for receiving." He started rummaging through a stack of folders on his desk. "I still got Chipman's file here—lemme check the date." He found the folder he wanted, started running his finger down the lengthy rap sheet inside it. "Here we go. March, 1932. What about it?"

"Since you boys are out looking for Pete Chipman, I'm assuming you talked to the brother, Duane?"

He gave me a stony look. He wasn't big on having his work questioned. "We would if we could find him. Came up empty on his address, job. No arrests after '32. Driving license expired three years back and never renewed."

"Have you pulled *his* arrest file from '32?"

"Didn't have no need for..." He gave me the dog eye. "What are you gettin' at?"

"Could we take a look at that file?"

He studied me under his bushy eyebrows for a minute before he picked up the phone.

***

When the clerk brought in the file, I snatched it out of her hand and flipped it open. The startled look she gave me turned to terror when Queenan shot to his feet.

"Hey! Get your mitts off that!" The woman made a quick retreat, and Queenan came around the desk and loomed over me. He held out a big bear paw. "Give it."

I'd already seen what I expected to see, so I handed it over. He sat down behind his desk with a huff. "You're gettin' a little too comfortable around here, Ross."

CHAPTER TWELVE

I held up my hands in surrender. "Sorry, couldn't resist. But take a look at the booking photo."

He glared at me for a second then spread the file open and looked it over. An interested look came into his eyes. "Kind of resembles our guy." He mused. "Younger version."

"Right," I said. "But that picture's seven years old." I took the mug shot he'd given me from the other Chipman file out of my pocket. "So's this one. Even though it looks just like the shitbird I've been running into. What strikes you as more likely..." I held the picture up, facing him. "That this guy hasn't changed in seven years?" I pointed at the folder on the desk. "Or that that guy looks like *this* now?"

He didn't answer. Just looked from one photo to the other and back again. After three or four times, he glanced up at me. "Well, there's an easy way to find out." He paged through the file, came out with a fingerprint card. He closed the folder and started pawing through the tall stack on his desk.

He slid out several other folders and stacked them on top of the first, then tapped the pile with a stubby digit. "The Jones shooting, the Rust kill, and just for giggles, I'll throw in your pal Vanner's case, too. I'm gonna run these over to Ray Pinker himself, and we'll see what we see."

"All right then." I got up. "What do you want me to do in the meantime?"

He lumbered to his feet and grabbed his hat off the rack. "I want you to get out of my office and out of my hair. I got work to do. And so do you." He bulldozed me out the door. "You keep beatin' the bushes, chase down all your cowboy pals, do whatever you gotta do, and let's find this son of a bitch." He winked. "But if I find him first, you owe me a bottle of Scotch."

"And what if I find him first?"

"You owe me *two* bottles."

* * *

I gave Bill Hart a call from my office. I was feeling a little guilty. What with all that had been going on of late, I'd almost forgotten I was supposed to be looking for his missing painting.

I brought him up to date on things as they stood. He knew about Dusty—Pooter had spoken to him—and he was horrified to hear that Dusty's shooting appeared to be connected to his missing painting. He told me he'd read about Rust's death in the papers and had wondered if it was connected. I didn't bother telling him about Jones's checkered past and what we'd learned, and hoped to learn, from the prison and arrest files. I figured once all the pieces fell into place, I could fill him in a little more. By then, he could probably read about it in the *Times*.

Since Gus was still out with the gout, I took Monte downstairs with me for an early lunch at the diner. Benjy asked how Dusty was doing and I told him what I could, which wasn't much. When I mentioned Walt, I was pleased to see that at least one other person in L.A. had no idea that Dusty had a son.

We went back upstairs, and I made a few phone calls, trying to find any sort of clue to help me locate Chipman. Central Casting didn't show him on a single call sheet since the day Jones was shot and had no address or telephone number for him on file. My pal Phil Okel, the security chief at Republic Pictures—which shot most of the better B westerns—knew Chipman's name only from seeing it on the occasional crew list. Phil's main contribution to my day was to regale me with a dirty limerick he'd just heard from his dentist. I'd heard it back in the days when I was still shooting marbles in the schoolyard.

I called a couple of rooming house managers I'd dealt with in the past who were among the few willing to rent to the notoriously rowdy cowboys. Nothing. Even my reliable pal Aggie could be no help. The paper's files had nothing on a Pete Chipman, not so much as a mention of his presence as a cast member on the day Jones was shot.

To give my dialing finger a break, I lit a cigar, poured myself a couple fingers of bourbon, and just sat back to think awhile. I was certain Chipman was still around. I'd encountered him twice already, and if he wanted Hart's painting bad enough to kill for it, he wasn't likely to fly the coop yet.

I was in mid-think when Monte sat bolt upright. He'd done it several times before when the phone was about to ring. I couldn't puzzle out how he knew, but sure enough, my phone started jangling. I reached for it, hoping that

CHAPTER TWELVE

maybe Aggie had turned up a line on Chipman. Also hoping it wasn't just Phil calling with another moldy limerick.

"Ross, it's Queenan." I winced. You had to hold the phone a foot from your head with him, or risk permanent damage. "How'd I know I'd find you sitting on your hams? I'm bettin' you got a bourbon in front of you—am I right?"

I covered my glass with a hand. I couldn't help it. "Just stopped in to make a few phone calls, Cap. Trying to get a bead on our boy." He sounded a little irritated, and I didn't get why he was giving me more than his usual dose of gaff.

"Look," he said. "I hate like hell to ever have to tell you that you done something right, especially twice in one week." *There* it was. "But damned if those prints we have for Duane Chipman don't tie him to the whole shebang. They're a solid match for the ones from the bar picture, the ones on Vanner's gun, a couple we found at Rust's place, and even the thumbprint on the brass from the round that killed Jones. We been lookin' for the wrong Chipman."

"Because Arizona's record says that Pete Chipman died there four years ago."

"Right. So I get your guy at the pen out there to wire me *his* prints, and bingo—they're a match for the ones we've got on file as Duane's. Just to cover bases, I pulled that expired driver's license of Duane Chipman's and what do you know—another perfect match to our crime scenes. 'Duane' is Pete, but Pete's dead, so Duane's our meat."

"How'd the mix-up happen?"

"Looks like somehow the dumb clucks workin' booking back in '32 managed to switch the names when they printed them. Sweet deal for our boy—once his big brother's jugged in Arizona, he's free to caper and leave all the prints he wants. Even more so after the brother croaked. We'd be looking for the wrong guy."

"Wasn't it in Pete's file that he'd been extradited to Arizona?"

"He wasn't. He was driving through Kingman and got picked up by the Arizona Highway Patrol off a wanted bulletin. I guess as part of his plea deal, he gave up his buddy Bianco, aka Jones. That's how Arizona come to put the snatch on *him* out here."

"So, now we know. Jones, Dusty, Rust—it's all been Duane Chipman."

"Yeah, but knowin' that don't help us find the prick. I'm puttin' out a bulletin of my own, and by dinner, I'll have every copper in the city on the lookout for this bird. Meanwhile, what are you gonna do?"

"If you're okay with it, I'm going to get the news out on the Gower Gulch grapevine that Chipman's good for both Jones and Rust. That ought to put their little feud to rest, and maybe one of them will give us something we can use. Somebody's bound to know where to find this guy."

"Hell, go ahead. Word's gonna get out soon enough, and it's not like, at this point, we're worried we're gonna spook him into hiding. But you got these yokels spread out from Simi to Indio, Lone Pine to Calexico, shootin' their horse operas. You think you can get the word spread that wide?"

"I can't, but I know somebody who can."

Chapter Thirteen

I took a short detour to the hospital to see about Dusty and to let Walt know his help had paid off in spades. The head nurse, a red-faced fireplug of a woman whose name tag read *Hilda*, corralled me before I got past the foyer and proceeded to give me a tongue-lashing about bringing my dog into a hospital. When I told her that the big animal belonged to Mr. Vanner in room 210, it didn't incline her to budge, so I went on to explain how distraught and sleepless the poor pup had been without his owner. I was laying it on heavy, and Monte chose that exact moment to lie down with his head on his paws and let out a whine—he does it when he's on a leash. She turned all dewy-eyed at that and said she supposed it would be all right this one time provided we didn't stay too long.

I promised her we wouldn't, and we got into the elevator. I looked down at the mutt, and he gave me a mischievous grin. I patted his head, "Bravo, Mr. Barrymore."

Other nurses tried to turn us around twice on our way down the long corridor, but when I told them that Hilda had given us a pass, they let us by without a fuss. Apparently, you didn't fool with Hilda.

Walt was coming out of Dusty's room in a rush, and we almost collided.

"There you are, Nate. I tried to call three times, but your line was busy. I was about to walk over to your office."

He was a little breathless, and my stomach did a barrel roll. "What's up?"

"He's awake. Awake and alert."

He ushered us in, and Dusty was sitting up in bed. He looked pale and tired, but his eyes were clear. He turned to look at us when we came in, and a wide smile fanned out under his big handlebar.

"Hey, there's my old amigo! And I see you brought Nate along with you."

Monte tugged me over, and if I hadn't held him back, he would have hopped right onto the bed with Dusty. He had to settle for some ear ruffling and chin scratching while he beat against my leg with his tail.

Dusty looked up from the dog to me. "It's good to see you, pard."

"You, too. It's about time you quit loafing. A lot's been going on while you were getting your forty winks."

"So I hear." He looked at Walt. "I'd make introductions, but I understand you boys have already met." Walt pushed a chair over next to the bed and motioned for me to sit. He took a chair on the other side and leaned an arm on the bed.

"Do you feel up to talking about it?" I asked Dusty.

"Hell, after the nap I've had I feel peppy as a ruttin' steer. I expect you want to know how I ended up here?"

"We can start there."

"It's all a little foggy." He sat up a little straighter. "I went into the office thinkin' I might find Pooter in there noodlin' over the books. He likes to do it when the place is shut up, and it's quiet. But the bar was a mess, and I could see we'd had a break-in. Then I was worried about Pooter, so I headed straight for the office. Soon as I walked in, something—or somebody, I guess—whacked me on the head, and I went down." He fiddled with a tube in his arm, and Walt batted his hand away.

"My head felt fuzzy for a while, and when it cleared a little, I got up off the floor, and there was a fellow standin' there pointin' a gun at me. My Colt." He gave his head an irritable shake. "My own damn gun. He had a bandana tied across his face like he was Jesse James or somethin'. If it wasn't for the mess out front and the lick on the head, I'd have thought it was somebody's idea of a joke."

"Did you recognize him?"

"No, he had a hat snugged down. I couldn't see nothin' but his eyes." He gave me a close look. "Why? Should I?"

I told him about Pete Chipman's prints being on his gun and on the Russell

CHAPTER THIRTEEN

print. I didn't mention the Rust and Jones developments. I didn't want to distract him.

"Well, I sure would have never figured him. I hardly know the man."

Likewise, I didn't tell him the Pete Chipman he thought he knew wasn't Pete Chipman.

"Did he say anything to you?"

His eyebrows bunched together while he thought. "He kept asking me, 'Where's it at?'" he said at last. "I didn't know what the hell he was talking about, and I told him so." He pinched his eyes shut. "Then he asked again and sort of waved the gun around the room while he did. When the muzzle was off me, that's when I went at him. We wrestled some, and he pushed me off..." He opened his eyes and looked up at the ceiling for a second, then shrugged and shook his head. "I don't remember nothin' after that. Sorry."

"Doesn't matter. He also left prints on that Russell picture you have behind the bar. Seems like what he was looking for was Bill Hart's painting."

"What painting?" I thought he was pulling my leg, but if the confusion on his face was an act, it was a good one. I looked at Walt. He shook his head and patted Dusty's arm.

"The doctor said your memory's apt to be a little patchy for a while, Pa. He said not to let it upset you—it'll straighten itself out in time."

"Well, that's a damned nuisance." Dusty sounded no more concerned than if he was remarking on the weather. He looked at me and repeated, "What painting?"

I laid the whole story out for him, and he had no recollection of our visits with Hart, or of our adventure up in the canyon.

"I can't figure why Chipman would think Pooter and me had something like that. Neither one of us knew Jones all that well—Pooter only took that side in the shooting 'cause he didn't like Rust. He wouldn't have touched something like that, anyway, and Jones and me bumped horns too many times for him to ask any favors of me. Hell, we had a little run-in at the Buscadero not two days before he died."

"What sort of run-in?"

"Aw, hell, he come swaggerin' in one night, fresh off the set and still wearin' his six-gun. You know we don't allow that—guns and drink are a bad mix. Especially the kind of drinking *he* did. So I told him he had to either hand it over or leave."

"What did he do?"

"He started to give me some lip, but then he seemed to think better of it. He unbuckled and handed 'er over—pistol, holster, money belt and all."

"Money belt?"

"Yeah, he always wore one of those old-timey money belt rigs." He described it with his hands as he went on. "Folded leather, stitched down the side with one end open, so's you could put coins and paper inside. The old-timers used to carry all their important papers in 'em, along with their cash."

Something stirred at the back of my brain. Hazel Rust came into my thoughts, and I started to replay the conversations we'd had. She'd mentioned thinking maybe Jones had hidden the painting away at a bus or train station. A locker, a claim check, something small.

"What did you do with it?" I asked Dusty.

"Locked it up in the office."

"Did he take it with him when he left?"

"I couldn't tell you. I don't recall when he left, but he didn't get it from me, anyway." He gave me a confused look. "Why does it matter? What are you thinkin'?"

"I'm thinking I need to go see your partner." I stood and picked up Monte's leash. "Come on, pal. Let's go see a man about a gun belt."

Walt got up and retrieved his hat from the bedside table. "Mind if I come with you?"

I aimed a thumb at my four-legged friend. "I'm still in the truck. If you don't mind sharing the seat with this guy…"

"Fine by me." He glanced at Dusty.

Dusty nodded and jerked his chin my way. "Go."

Walt went out the door ahead of us. I was in the doorway when I heard behind me "Nate." I turned to look at the old cowboy in the bed.

He pointed a finger at me like a gun. "You look out for my boy, you hear me?"

CHAPTER THIRTEEN

The drive over was a trial for all three of us. Me, because the driver's window in Arnie's truck had no crank, and without the air flow, the heat—never mind the dog breath—was stifling. Monte, because he was stuck in the middle and not able to hang his head out the passenger window the way he was used to doing. Plus, I couldn't shift gears without jabbing my elbow into his chest. Walt, meanwhile, was jammed against the passenger door because the big hound, in true canine fashion, insisted on taking up his share of the seat and then some.

We were so crammed together that when I parked at the curb and we opened our doors, Walt and I both popped out like clowns from a jack-in-the-box. It was moderately busy in the bar, so much so that Pooter skipped his customary greeting and just gave us a tilt of his chin and a cheerful, "Hey boys," as he carried half a dozen beers, three mug handles in each fist, to a group of cowboys at a back table. From the sound of them, it wasn't their first round.

The crowd wasn't what it would be later, but cowboys among their own are never quiet. Between half a dozen high-spirited conversations going on at once and the Bob Wills swing tune blaring out of the big Symphonola jukebox, the din seemed to vibrate the whole place like an aftershock.

Pooter made his way back over to where we stood. He gave Monte a pat or two while he raised his voice over the racket. "Somethin' to drink, boys?"

I shook my head and leaned in closer so I wouldn't have to bellow. "Can we talk in your office?"

He gave me a worried look, but nodded and tapped a tall, lanky guy sitting at the bar on the shoulder. "Mind the till, will you, Len?" The beanpole left his stool, went behind the bar, and struck an official pose, to general laughter from the room.

Pooter led us back to the office and closed the door. It didn't block out all the noise, but we could at least talk without shouting at each other.

Pooter looked tense, and his eyes shifted from Walt to me and back. Before I could say anything, he asked, "Everything all right with Dusty?"

"He's better, Uncle Gerald." Walt put a hand on his shoulder. "He's awake now and talking. The doctors say he's going to be just fine."

Pooter blew out a breath, and his shoulders sagged with relief. "Well, that's welcome news. If I can get ol' Len out there to spell me awhile longer, I'll head on over there and see him." He looked at me. "But right now, you boys are looking like there's something else on your mind."

I nodded. "Dusty tells me that a couple days before he was shot dead, Ty Jones came in wearing his gun, and Dusty took it from him, rig and all."

He looked surprised. "Huh. News to me—he never mentioned it."

"So Jones didn't get it back from you?"

"Nope. This is the first I'm hearin' of it."

"Where would he have put something like that?"

"In the bottom desk drawer if he was plannin' to give it back right away. We've had to collect a few here and there, especially since that mess with Leo Rust. If the boy's tipped one too many, we lock 'em up in the safe, and they can reclaim 'em the next day."

"There's no chance Jones's was in there the night Dusty was shot?"

Pooter shook his head. "No, I took the receipts home that night, so I left the safe standin' open. And just the day before, I'd got a pistol and belt out of there for Sandy Dowd, and there wasn't no other in there."

I recalled the cowboy I'd seen in the bar the other day, leaving with a rolled-up gun belt. "Is he a little blond guy, was in here with Joe Lopez?"

"That's him."

"What did it look like?"

"The gun? Just the usual Colt. Frontier model, wood handles. Nothin' fancy."

"And the leather?"

"Nice saddle leather holster. Soft belt with cartridge loops across the back. Holster had a fancy concho on it."

"Soft belt. Like a money belt, maybe?"

"Could've been. It was rolled up tight, so…"

I still carried Hart's found concho in my pocket. I showed it to Pooter. "The concho…was it anything like that?"

"Yessir, just like that."

Before we left I told Pooter and the boys in the bar that Chipman was good

CHAPTER THIRTEEN

not only for Rust, but for Jones and Dusty, too. Chipman wasn't likely to have any friends once that word got around, and they promised to get it traveling.

Chapter Fourteen

Sandy Dowd, according to a couple of the cowboys, was staying in a rooming house only a couple of miles away. We piled back into the pickup and drove over. I found the house with no trouble. It was in a so-so neighborhood north of Santa Monica Boulevard. The house was a mid-sized two-story Victorian in sore need of upkeep with a small, railed porch and a little patch of half-dead grass in front. Judging from the row of mailboxes attached to the wall beside the front door, there were four rooms being let out.

This sort of layout didn't lend itself to the usual breaking and entering, if it came to that. Too confined, too much common area, too much chance of being noticed. Anyway, the gang at the Buscadero had told us the only local thing doing that day was a singing cowboy picture Republic was shooting out in Chatsworth, and it had finished midday. Dowd had been on that set there, so he wasn't working out of town. I was hoping we'd find him at home or coming home. Not that I wanted to brace him. Not yet.

"So, what are you thinking?" Walt asked as I drove past the house. "That this Dowd was working with Pete Chipman?"

"I'm thinking there are two possibilities. One, that Dowd's been in this caper since the beginning. And the other, that Dowd has no clue what he has." The boys who had given me Dowd's address said they'd noticed him wearing Jones's gun rig on the set that day. Nobody had asked him about it, but it had caused some fresh grumbling among the Rust/Jones factions. "News travels fast on the cowboy telegraph," I said. "If Chipman's heard that Dowd has that gun belt, partner or not he'll be coming around for it. Either

CHAPTER FOURTEEN

way, odds are good he'll show up here." And I *was* looking forward to bracing *him*.

First order of business was to find out which room was Dowd's. I drove two blocks up, turned down a side street, and stopped. "You ready to cut your teeth on a little real-life private eye work?" I asked Walt.

"Absolutely." He leaned back to see me around the mutt's huge noggin and gave me an eager smile. "What do I need to do?"

I held out the end of the leash. "Take Monte for a walk."

The enthusiasm left his face. "You're serious? Walk your dog?"

"This guy's seen me at the bar. I don't know if he'd know who I am, but I don't want to take the chance. Walk Monte down the block, then take him up on the lawn near the bushes along the porch. He'll know what to do there. While he's doing it, you should be able to lamp the mailboxes and see which one's Dowd's."

He looked skeptical, but he took the leash. He fished a pair of steel-rimmed sunglasses from his pocket, put them on, and they got out of the truck. I watched them in the mirror as they rounded the corner, Monte's big plume tail waving. Much as he hated the leash, he was always game for a walk.

It was fifteen minutes before they came around the corner again. Walt was looking amused and pretty pleased with himself as they got back in the truck.

"What took you so long? Monte not holding up his end?"

"Oh, no," he said with a chuckle. "He did just fine. But while he was giving the hedge a nice, long soaking, the old lady who runs the place came out to yell at us." He chuckled again. "Hell, that's probably the most watering those bushes have had all year."

"Did you get a look at the mailboxes?"

"Better." He laughed once again. "When she noticed my sunglasses, she started getting fluttery and tongue-tied. 'Oh, I'm so sorry, mister,' she said. 'I didn't know he was one of *those* dogs.' Long story short, she invited me into the parlor for a lemonade. I saw the mailboxes, and I got a look up the inside stairs. Dowd's in room two, on the west side, front corner."

"Not bad for a greenhorn," I said as I dropped the truck into gear. "If the lawyering racket doesn't work out, you just might make a detective."

I u-turned and took the corner, pulling to the curb well up the block from the house. We had a full view from there of the front and most of the west side. Dowd's being a corner room, there were windows on two sides. A shade was half open behind the west-side window and I didn't see any lights on inside.

"Now, what do we do?"

"The worst part of my racket," I said. "We wait. And watch."

It wasn't an ideal setup for a stakeout. Not that Arnie's eyesore of a pickup looked out of place in that neighborhood, but I wasn't sure two guys in jackets and neckties sitting in it with a dog wouldn't draw some notice. We did what we could. We both stripped off coats and ties and rolled up our sleeves. I found a greasy cap under my seat and slapped it on, hoping I wouldn't end up with lice. We were as inconspicuous as we could possibly be with the large red mutt occupying half the seat between us.

After two hours of nothing happening, we were all getting restless and hungry. I was debating whether to leave Walt and Monte to do their blind man-guide dog act while I went to pick up some sandwiches and coffee, or to have Walt take the truck since I knew our two birds by sight and take the chance they'd spot me first.

While I mulled over the issue, a dusty, much abused Buick sedan came rattling down the street in our direction. It pulled to a stop in front of the rooming house with a loud squealing of tires against curbstone. The driver was a bottle-blond dolly wearing neon bright red lipstick and too much of it. I couldn't see the passenger from my angle, but when the door creaked open and he half stepped, half tumbled out I recognized the man of the hour, Sandy Dowd.

"This is him," I told Walt. "Take a good look." Walt nodded and watched as Dowd, who'd fallen to one knee with a curse, lumbered back up and swiped with both hands at the smudged knee of his dungarees. His blond hair was ruffled, and he reached up and felt at it before diving back into the car with a laugh and coming out with a sweat-stained tan Stetson, which he plunked down on his head, backward.

He and the girl exchanged boozy goodbyes and a few words I couldn't hear,

CHAPTER FOURTEEN

then he banged the door shut and watched her drive more or less straight up the street and out of sight. He looked around for a moment as if he was unsure which house was his, then made his unsteady way up the cracked walk and, after a couple of practice tries, up the three steps to the porch. He managed to get through the door on the first try, and a minute or so later, I saw a light come on in his room. I'd noted that he wasn't wearing or carrying a gun belt. It made me wish I'd chanced going into his place before. I only hoped he hadn't already handed it off to Chipman.

The shade came down, and I saw a flicker or two of shadow behind it, then nothing. Twenty minutes later, the light went out.

"So now what?" Walt asked.

Dusk was full on by then. I'd decided I didn't want to leave Walt alone in case Chipman put in an appearance. With my flimsy disguise and darkness coming on, I figured I was safe enough from detection, so taking Monte with me, I got out. I gave Walt five bucks and directions to a drive-in diner not more than a mile away.

I walked Monte up the block and down to the other end. A tall hedge around the bend at the corner house offered good cover but left me a decent view of Dowd's place. I lit a cigar and leaned on a public mailbox to continue the watching and waiting. Monte sat beside my feet and faced the opposite way, keeping a lookout behind me. An ideal assistant, and he worked cheap.

Nothing was stirring in the neighborhood, so I didn't feel any need to keep moving. Half an hour later headlights approached me along the side street we were on, and Monte stood up, alert. I started him down the walk toward the headlights, trying to look natural—just a regular joe out walking the dog. Closer to the headlights, I picked up the familiar clack of a straight six engine with a burned valve. Walt had circled around on his way back with the food so as not to drive past the rooming house again. The guy learned fast.

I parked the pickup in the same spot as before and we sat sipping coffee and eating pastramis—a hamburger with no trimmings for Monte. Just to pass the time we started swapping stories of our youth. Walt talked about what it was like living as a virtual orphan, with a mother gone and a father he saw for a few days a year if he was lucky. I described growing up with a father you idolized, only to find out too late he wasn't the man you always thought he was. I told him about my time with the sheriffs, and how testifying against a few bent badges had driven a wedge not only between me and my cop brotherhood, but between my old man and me. I figured that, being in the legal game himself, he might understand. He admitted that he'd already heard most of the story from Pooter. He didn't say it outright, but I thought he must have approved, or he wouldn't be sitting there then, offering me what help he could.

Monte had curled up and had gone to sleep, taking up even more of the seat but making us at least a little less conspicuous. Walt and I agreed to take turns ourselves, one sleeping while the other kept watch. We'd planned to do it in two-hour shifts, but I didn't think either of us slept more than a half an hour at a time.

During my turns watching, the occasional car passed us by or came or went at one of the other houses. But no one seemed to notice us, and I didn't see anything that raised a flag. We each took a break about midway through the night to slip out and visit those tall hedges on the corner and rid ourselves of the coffee we'd drunk. The dome light bulb in the truck was helpfully burned out, so we were able to come and go without notice.

* * *

Around 5:30 sunlight was creeping over the hills and people started coming out here and there from the houses around us and driving off to jobs or wherever else the new day took them. I was about to move the truck to a different vantage point when I saw light appear behind Dowd's window shades.

I could see vague movements behind the shades, and fifteen minutes later, the light went out again. Shortly after, Dowd stepped out onto the porch wearing the same clothes as before but looking sober, shaved, and rested. He wasn't wearing a gun belt, but he carried a bundle tucked underneath his arm. It looked like a denim work jacket with something heavy and bulky rolled up in it. He stepped down the walkway and headed up the sidewalk away

CHAPTER FOURTEEN

from us with the cowboy's typical swaggering gait, whistling as he walked.

I nudged Walt awake. "Our boy's on the move." He rubbed the sleep out of his eyes and watched Dowd head up the street.

"No sign of Chipman?"

"Nothing." When Dowd crossed at the end of the block, I started the truck, and Monte popped up with a yawn.

I waited while a blue coupe passed us, then eased out behind it and followed Dowd up the street. Three blocks up, I pulled to the curb again, and we watched him board a red car at the stop on Santa Monica Blvd. I waited until the car got underway, then made a left onto the boulevard and followed the tracks east. The early morning traffic was thick enough that I was able to keep two or three cars between us and the streetcar. I wasn't too concerned—Dowd hadn't shown any sign he suspected a tail, and I hadn't spotted anyone else following him. I had a pretty good notion of where he was headed. I was sure of it when he got off the car at Vine and started walking north.

Following him up Vine was a cinch. The light foot traffic would have made him easy to keep a bead on even if he hadn't been the only guy on the street topped by a cowboy hat. It became trickier after he made the turn at Sunset. The closer he got to Gower, the more similar headgear we saw. When he reached the corner and the drugstore, he was swallowed up in a throng of cowboys, all dressed in some version of their trade's uniform—big felt hat, plaid shirt, wide cuffed dungarees, tall boots. The variations were slight—some wore vests, some wore bandanas, a few wore chaps. But overall, the look was so standard that trying to pick Dowd out from a distance was like looking for a needle in a box of needles.

"Shit. I didn't count on this." I pulled us over half a block away and cut the engine.

Walt craned his neck and scanned the crowd milling on the sidewalk and spilling over the curb. "I've lost him in that bunch," he said. "Can you see him?"

"No." I'd never been here at this time in the morning, before most of the boys dispersed after lining up work for the day. I'd seen it crowded, but I judged that we were looking at four or five times the group we'd found when

Walt and I had come here before.

I thought I knew most of the day-playing cowboys—at least by sight—from seeing them at the Buscadero, but looking them over, I noticed quite a few unfamiliar faces. Picking out individual cowboys was difficult since most of them continually moved from one knot of gabbing men to another or drifted in and out of the drugstore.

I wasn't concerned about Chipman showing up there. Word was spreading by now that he was responsible for both Jones and Rust, so either side would be bound to make things warm for him if he showed his face. Even if he did, my odds of singling him out among all these lookalikes were pretty thin.

"You don't think Chipman's likely to turn up here, do you?" Walt asked, echoing my thoughts. I just shook my head and kept my eyes on the crowd. "So, what should we do now?"

I thought it over for a minute. "We've already talked to most of these guys," I said. "So they already know we're looking for Chipman. But only Pooter and a couple of the boys know we were asking about Dowd, so maybe that hasn't gotten around yet." I got out of the truck, and Monte started to follow. "You stay here, boy," I told him. He wasn't happy about it, but he took up his post in the middle of the seat again.

I walked around to talk to Walt through the window. "Stay here with him, will you? I'm going in there. If anybody asks me, I'm still trying to get help finding Chipman. Who knows—I may get more cooperation now. But I want to see if I can spot Dowd, see who he's talking to. It could be there are even more people involved in this thing than we know."

"What if he sees you?"

"Again, I'm not sure he knows me, but if he does, I'm sure he's heard that I'm asking after Chipman. He should have no reason to think I'm looking for him. Meanwhile, keep your eyes open for the guy. If he shows before I come back, just try and see where he goes."

"Will do," He shot Monte a doubtful look. "Is he going to be all right here with just me?"

"The guy who fed him steak? You're pals for life now. It'll be safer for you than for anybody who bothers you." I handed him the truck keys. "Just in

CHAPTER FOURTEEN

case." I started to go, then checked myself. "But don't go driving off without me."

* * *

I drew some curious looks and a few friendly hellos as I weaved my way through the mass of men crowding the sidewalk the whole length of the Columbia Drugstore. I kept my eyes moving as I went along, trying to spot Dowd and especially keeping an eye out for that blue bundle that he'd been carrying. More than a couple of the boys stopped me to ask if what they'd heard about Pete Chipman was true and, when I said that it was, to wish me luck tracking him down. Pooter and the boys had done their part. But nobody offered any helpful information about Chipman. I kept these conversations as short as I could. I didn't want to get distracted and miss Dowd.

As crowded as the sidewalk was, it was the wide-open spaces compared to the crush of bodies inside the drugstore. Canned sardines enjoyed more elbow room. The clamor from all the yammering cowboys was almost as bad as Saturday nights at the Buscadero. I felt like I was wading through fresh-poured concrete as I made my way from the front door toward the pay phone near the back of the store. It was the epicenter of activity at Gower Gulch, in constant use as news about jobs for the day, or preferably longer, went out and came in. It also served as the personal line for cowboys who couldn't afford a home phone, although you tied it up for more than two or three minutes at your peril.

The mob grew even thicker, and the din louder, the closer I came to the phone. The bodies were so tightly bunched there that about all I could make out around it was the tops of hats. And nearly every one of those was a copy of Dowd's own dusty tan, well-worn, ten-gallon topper.

I'd just about concluded I was wasting my time there and had decided to start swimming upstream toward the door, when on the other side of the store a black hat caught my eye. Under it, I made out the familiar face of Joe Lopez, who'd been with Dowd when I'd seen the young cowboy at the Buscadero. Joe kept up as well as anyone with Gower Gulch gossip but, unlike his buckaroo brethren. You could always count on him to keep a thing on the q.t.

I inched my way toward where Joe stood talking to another cowboy at the end of the lunch counter. When I was halfway there, he looked up and caught sight of me, and I signaled that I wanted to talk to him. He nodded his understanding and pointed his chin toward a rear corner of the store. I started moving in that direction, and after sharing a last word or two with the guy at the counter, Joe did the same. When we met at the back, he led me down a short hallway, and we stepped through a curtained doorway into a small storage room. It was no quieter behind the flimsy curtain, but we could at least talk without being overheard.

"I'm guessing this is somethin' to do with Pete Chipman," Joe said before I'd gotten a word out.

"Not exactly. Well, in a way, it is. But I need you to keep this under the hat. For now, anyway."

"Sure thing."

"I'm looking for the guy I saw you at the bar with the other day. Sandy Dowd."

Joe looked puzzled. "What for? He's a green kid, fresh off his daddy's horse ranch up the coast. He ain't been in town but a month or two. I'm not sure he even knows Pete Chipman."

"Maybe not, but I think he's got something Chipman's been after. And if I'm right, it's what Ty Jones and Leo Rust died over. And what Dusty was damned near killed for."

His face darkened at that. Feelings might have been split over Rust and Jones, but Dusty was another matter.

"I don't get it," he said. "What could Chipman want from a young'un like Sandy?"

"Ty Jones's gun rig."

Joe scoffed. "Hell, Nate, that thing ain't worth much. It's decent leather and all, but the pistol's nothin' special. It's nothin' to kill anyone over."

"Why did Dowd want it, then? He told Pooter it was his."

"Aw, the little jughead. He didn't have a rig of his own, and you know how

CHAPTER FOURTEEN

we get paid a little kicker if we bring our own gear onto a picture. We were both there the night Dusty collected it from Ty, and then he went and got shot before he ever reclaimed it. Ty had told everybody he didn't have any family, so the kid figured there was no harm if he took it. I thought he was out of line, but I wasn't going to inform on him." He shrugged. "To be honest, I wasn't any too fond of Ty Jones myself."

"If that's the case, Joe, the kid might be in danger. I don't have time to get into why right now, but Chipman's after that rig, and trust me, he'll do whatever it takes to get his mitts on it. Can you help me find Dowd? All those tan hats out there look alike to me."

"Well, hell, you just missed him. He took a phone call right after he walked in here, and he left out the back door."

"He say where he was going?"

"Not to me. He's been runnin' around with a secretary he met over at Monogram. I figured he was probably off to see her."

I thought about the lipstick blonde I'd seen at Dowd's place. "How long ago?"

"Not five minutes." He jerked a thumb over his shoulder. "She works in their offices right around the corner. You might catch up with him there. Need me to come along?"

"No, I've got help, thanks. But if Dowd comes back, try to get him to stick around. He'll be safe enough here."

"Okay, will do."

"Thanks, pal. I owe you a beer."

Chapter Fifteen

I stepped through the curtain and went out the back door at the end of the hall. It opened onto a parking lot shared by the drugstore and several of the surrounding buildings, most of which belonged to the various small production companies that kept the Gower Gulch gang employed.

Kitty-corner across the lot I could see the top of a tall studio building that fronted on Beachwood Drive, the next block over. "Reliable Studios" was painted in fading letters on the wall facing me, but I knew from Dusty that Monogram had taken over Reliable a couple years back. I started across the lot in that direction. A narrow alley ran between two of the buildings and emptied on to Beachwood. If Dowd was headed to Monogram, it would be the most likely route.

When I was fifty feet from the mouth of the alley, I heard what sounded like somebody running. As I got closer, I was sure they were running feet, more than one person from the sound of it, and they were headed my way. Before I could decide how to play it, a gunshot boomed and echoed through the alley, followed by a cry of pain. That decided me.

I drew my .380 and took a quick peek around the corner. Sandy Dowd was lying maybe thirty feet down the alley. He was moaning and had both hands clasped around his left leg. The blue denim bundle was on the ground next to him, and coming up the alley, a big blue automatic in his hand, was Pete Chipman.

Chipman's jaw was set. He was looking at Dowd and raising the gun to fire again when he caught sight of me and sent a wild shot my way. I fired back, and he ducked behind a skid of bricks sitting against one of the buildings. I

CHAPTER FIFTEEN

used that chance to edge my way along the wall to where Dowd was down. He looked up at me, first with a flash of fear in his eyes, then with confused recognition.

I grabbed him by the collar and dragged him toward a recessed doorway that looked deep and wide enough to offer us cover. He pushed with his good leg to help me along, and I'd just gotten him to safety when Chipman ducked around the bricks and sent two more shots our way. I was about to shoot back when his head disappeared behind the bricks again, so I held my fire.

The kid was bunched up on his side in the corner of the alcove, both legs drawn up. With shaking hands, he tied a bandana around his wounded leg, just below the knee. He winced and hissed with pain as he pulled it tight.

"You okay, kid?"

He didn't answer, but his eyes flicked up at me, and he gave me a quick, nervous nod.

I aimed at the spot where Chipman's head had appeared and waited for another chance. We were about twenty-five yards apart, and I thought my odds of hitting him were better than even. But instead of obliging me with an appearance, he called out from his hiding spot.

"I know who you are, Mister. Dusty's private eye friend. I've got no quarrel with you. Just leave me that package your young friend was carrying, and we can go our separate ways."

I'd forgotten for the moment about Dowd's bundle. It was lying too far away for me to try for it but was even further out of Chipman's reach.

"Come on, detective man," he yelled. "Don't nobody need to get hurt here."

"Tell that to this kid with the bullet in his leg."

Without warning, he popped up above the stacked bricks and potted another round at me. It clipped the wall above my head and sprinkled my hat with concrete and stucco dust. I snapped a quick return shot and heard him yelp.

Before we could throw any more lead at each other, I heard a rumble and a madly tooting horn behind me. I looked back to see Arnie's disreputable pickup barreling across the parking lot and beelining for the alley. I caught a glimpse of Walt behind the wheel, looking grim and determined and more like his old man than he ever had.

He gave the horn a few more blasts as the truck bounced into the alley and ground to a stop twenty feet past us and directly over Dowd's bundled jacket. I heard noise from Chipman's direction and turned to see him running back down the alley, his right hand with the gun still in it pressed against his left shoulder.

"Monte, stay!" I yelled as the big red dog was climbing out the window to go in pursuit. He gave me a disappointed look and sat back. I couldn't get a shot at Chipman with the truck blocking my way. He turned near the end of the alley and sent a parting shot our way, which hit the truck with a thunk. I heard a hiss and gurgle and saw that the bullet had punched a hole in the radiator.

"Well, shit." I looked at Walt. "Take care of the kid, all right?" I ran down the alley and came out the other end only to see Chipman on a dark red motorcycle disappearing into the distance. When I got back to the truck, Walt was doing what he could to tend to Dowd, while Monte looked on.

"How'd you two end up here?" I asked Walt. He answered me over his shoulder while he pressed a handkerchief against Dowd's blood-soaked bandana.

"We were waiting for you to come back when I recognized Chipman riding past us on a motorcycle. I saw him turn down at the corner, so I got out to try and see where he went. I saw him park the bike and go into the alley, and it looked like he might be headed your way."

"Well, that was a hell of an entrance you two made."

He pulled up the edge of the bandana. "Could be worse," he told Dowd. "It looks like it just hit the meat."

Dowd looked up at me. "Thanks, mister. I'd have been in a bad way if you hadn't come along."

"What the hell were you doing out here with him?" I asked. I was inclined to believe Joe Lopez about the kid, but every now and then, I'm wrong.

"I don't even know the man," he said. "I mean, I've seen him around, but..." He angled a chin toward the drugstore. "I got a phone call that said if I ever wanted to see Doris—that's my girl, she works just down the way." He pointed

CHAPTER FIFTEEN

toward the Monogram building. "They told me if I ever wanted to see her alive again, to come to her office lickety-split." He gave me a weak smile. "Just some of the boys having fun with the new fella, I thought. But I figured I might as well head over and let 'em have their joke."

He looked down the alley. "Then he popped out of a doorway down there, and as soon as I saw that gun, I knew it was no joke. So I started running. What the hell's he want to rob me for, anyway? I ain't got any money."

I got down and dragged his bundled jacket out from under the truck. "He was after what you had in here."

I spread the jacket on the ground and lifted out the holstered pistol with the belt wrapped tightly around it. It was a handsome piece of leatherwork, well-worn but nicely tooled, and dyed a deep tobacco brown. The concho on the holster was a smaller version of the ones on Jones's chaps. The pistol, as described, was an ordinary Colt single action, the same as nearly every Hollywood cowboy favored on screen or off. This one had seen some rough use—its once-blue finish had worn away to a dull, steel wool gray, and the wood grips were cracked and chipped.

Dowd looked at me like I was pulling his leg. His good leg. "Why would he want to shoot me over that? Hell, you could buy a better setup than that one, six gun and all, for twenty bucks at any pawn shop."

"Maybe so, but I think this one's got a special attraction." Dowd, Walt, and even Monte, watched with curious interest as I slipped the holstered revolver off and held the belt up by the buckle end. I could see that it was folded on itself and stitched down to create one long, narrow pocket. I stuck a couple of fingers in the opening behind the buckle and came out with a folded piece of paper. I opened it up and looked it over, then showed it to Walt.

"Parole ticket for one Tirone Bianco. I guess Arizona and California can both scratch him off the books now." I stuck the paper in my pocket and poked around inside the belt some more but couldn't see or feel anything else. I took it by the other end, held it upside down, and started shaking it. On the third shake, a small yellow rectangle of paper slipped out and fluttered to the ground. I picked up the thing that had gotten Jones and Rust—and almost gotten Dusty, Dowd, and me—killed. And all I could do was laugh and shake my head. I looked down at Dowd. "Funny you should mention pawn shops, kid."

* * *

The ambulance crew wouldn't let me ride with Dowd. I wanted to question him some more, and I knew that once the doctors got their rubber-gloved mitts on him, it would be hours, at least, before I could talk to him. What little I'd gotten from him so far was nothing I didn't already know, but it made me more inclined to agree with Joe—Dowd was just a hayseed kid who had no clue what he'd walked into.

I'd made three phone calls from the drugstore—one for the ambulance, one to fill Queenan in and get my ear gnawed off, and one to Pooter asking if he'd be willing to hold on to Monte for a while. Since the truck was out of commission, we found a taxi at a stand near the corner. The driver balked at letting a dog ride in his cab, and I had to hand him a five-spot for a convincer. On the way to the hospital, we detoured over to the Buscadero to drop Monte off.

The receiving hospital was next door to the Hollywood station, and Queenan was waiting for us when we got there. He was standing on the sidewalk out front with two other detectives and waved us over as we were going inside.

"Your boy's already in surgery," he said. "So you can stay here and tell me all about your latest fiasco." He turned to his two companions. "Boys, meet the infamous Nate Ross, the concrete cowboy. Private eye, disturber of the public peace, and perpetual pain in my ass."

Before I could conjure up a witty comeback, he went on. "Detectives Deacon and Valverde here couldn't wait to meet you, seeing as how you've been keepin' 'em so busy as of late."

Both coppers stifled grins and nodded curt hellos, but neither one spoke. Walt stepped forward and broke the silence. "Detectives, good to see you again."

Valverde gave another nod. "Mr. Vanner."

CHAPTER FIFTEEN

Queenan's eyebrows shot up. "Vanner? Holy hell, we got two of 'em runnin' around town?"

"Walter *VanNeer*," Walt said, sticking out a hand, which Queenan shook with some suspicion. "Dusty's my father."

Queenan looked him up and down, taking in the tailored suit. "You ain't a cowboy, too, I hope."

"Attorney," Walt said with a smile.

"Good God all Friday!" Queenan jabbed his cigar in my direction. "Although the way this joker runs his racket, it ain't a half bad idea for him to travel around with a lawyer."

Once Queenan got started listing my shortcomings, I knew he could go on for quite a while, so I spoke up to change the subject. "Is the girl all right?"

Queenan eyeballed me for a second before he answered. "She's aces," he said irritably. Probably annoyed I cut his comedy act short. "I sent a couple of uniforms over to check on her. Found her workin' behind her desk like normal. No idea she'd been used to bait your cowboy pal out into the open. Threw quite a winging when they told her he was shot, though. They're gonna drive her over here soon as she's calmed down enough."

As if on cue, a patrol car pulled to the curb and stopped. Before the two coppers inside could even get their caps on, the girl I'd seen at Dowd's place bailed out, wailing. Her lipstick was smeared, and stripes of mascara ran down both her cheeks like war paint. She ran past us without seeming to see us, up the few concrete steps and into the building.

The two bluesuits walked over to where we stood, looking sheepish. The older of the pair, a beefy, red-faced bird with eyebrows so blond they were nearly white, stuck a finger under his hat and scratched. "I don't know how much you'll get out of her, Cap. She hasn't said a sensible word since we told her the boyfriend got pinked."

"Well, it don't sound like there's much more to get," Queenan said. "But we gotta try." He turned to Deacon and Valverde. "You boys want to go sheep dog Betty Boop? Maybe once the doctor tells her the kid in there ain't gonna croak, she'll be able to put a sentence or two together." He waved the cigar toward Walt and me. "I'll talk to these two, get the other side of this thing."

He looked at the uniforms. "And you two can get out there and join the hunt. We gotta run this Chipman bird to ground—he's shot enough people around here already."

The two detectives went inside, and the patrol coppers drove off.

"Come on," Queenan turned toward the police station. "It's too warm to stand around talkin' in the sun."

* * *

Queenan rocked back in his chair, propped a foot against the desktop, and chewed his cigar without saying anything. I knew the move—it was supposed to make us uneasy. He knew me well enough to know it was wasted on me, so it had to be for Walt's benefit. But Walt looked perfectly at ease, sitting in the chair to my right with legs crossed and both hands resting on his knee. Cops don't spook lawyers.

"So," Queenan said at last, "Mr. Vanner—excuse me, *VanNeer*—you've only been in town a few days and your pal here has managed to plop you right in the middle of your standard Nate Ross bucket o'worms. Lucky you."

Walt didn't take the bait. He just sat there, giving Queenan a neutral gaze. I wanted to hurry things along—I had an important errand to run—so I spoke up.

"All we were doing was trying to find Chipman, Cap, just like you told me to."

"I don't remember telling you to get in no shootouts at high noon."

"He'd shot the kid. He was about to finish the job. Then he shot at me. What was I supposed to do? If I'd had a phone handy, I would have rung you up on the spot so he could shoot at you instead."

"The kid," Queenan repeated. "See, that's the thing. You've been playin' patty-cake with me since this whole thing started. I'm supposed to tell you everything, while you tell me nothin'. You always keep an ace up your sleeve and expect me not to call you out for cheatin'."

"What ace up my sleeve?"

"Let me play Nate Ross for a minute and answer your question with

CHAPTER FIFTEEN

more questions. What's this kid, Dowd got to do with Chipman? What did Chipman want from him? And what's this art theft caper you claim you been workin' really all about? 'Cause from where I sit, it sure don't look like no *petty* theft."

I blew out a long breath. "I'd tell you if I could, Cap. I would. But I made my client a promise."

He dropped his foot to the floor, leaned in to slap the desktop, and let out a howl of laughter. "A promise? Since when have you started keepin' promises? You've sure as hell never kept one you gave *me*."

"Come on, Cap, that's bullshit, and you know it. Besides, you really ought to be thanking me on this one."

"Thanking you?" He leaned forward a little more, and the veins in his neck started to swell. "Thanking you for what exactly?"

"Gee, I don't know. How about for finding your mystery man in the Jones kill? For identifying Rust's killer? For tying Dusty's shooting to Chipman? For stopping another murder in your backyard? If it wasn't for me, you boys might still be running around looking for a guy who's been dead for four years."

He started to speak, but just made a strangled sound deep in his throat. The neck veins threatened to burst, and I considered taking cover so I wouldn't get sprayed. I glanced at Walt, and he still sat in the same attitude with the same impassive expression. There was a little gleam in his eye, like he was enjoying the show.

Finally, Queenan sat back and took a long, deep breath. He picked up his cigar and took a pull at it, but it had gone cold. He threw it over his shoulder in disgust and looked at me.

"You got some stones, mister. Nobody can say you don't. So you ain't gonna tell me what you're up to. All right, since you know so much, how do you think I should deal with *that*?"

I knew I was on thinner ice than usual with him and that I had to step carefully. "I think you should chalk up your wins here and send me on my way, Cap."

"And why would I do that?"

"Because if you don't, you risk never bagging Chipman at all or getting to the bottom of all this. But if you do, I'm leaving you with my promise…" I raised a hand. "My solemn promise, that I'll give you answers to those questions just as soon as I can."

He stared at me for a long time. As he stared, he slowly fished a fresh cigar out of his coat pocket and trimmed it carefully with his little pen knife. He took his time lighting it, turning it slowly in the flame.

Now, I *was* getting uneasy. Queenan was never so fearsome as when he was calm. When he spoke. His voice was so cool and even that it gave me a chill.

"I'm gonna hold you to that. Now get the hell out of my office."

Chapter Sixteen

The sign above the plate glass window read "Golden State Loans" in big, dignified Old English letters. The same style of lettering appeared in gold leaf on the large window itself and on the half window in the impressive carved oak door. If the window had been curtained, passersby might have imagined beyond that curtain a paneled office with a rich carpet, deep and soft as beach sand, and a huge mahogany desk with a solemn-faced old bird in wing collar and spats behind it, eager to expound on interest rates and amortization. But the odd assortment of jewelry, clocks and watches, typewriters, guns, banjos, bicycles, and all manner of gimcracks and geegaws displayed behind the glass showed Golden State Loans for what it was—a run of the mill hock shop.

And nobody would ever mistake the fellow behind the glass counter—no mahogany desk in sight—for J. P. Morgan. A sour-faced, bald-domed guy of fifty or so in a ratty brown cardigan, he'd have looked more at home shooting craps in a Spring Street alley than sipping sherry at the Jonathan Club.

He was wiping said counter with a dirty rag when I walked in, and he looked up at the tinkling of the bell above the door. He stuffed the rag in a back pocket and shuffled out to meet me halfway across the cracked linoleum.

"What can we do for you today, friend?" He had a wheezy voice with an east of the Rockies twinge to it. Chicago, maybe Detroit. He looked me over with a pawnbroker's natural suspicion. From the deference in his greeting, I was guessing he pegged me as a detective on the pawn shop squad.

"You the owner?"

He hesitated before he answered, like he'd thought I was asking a trick question. "That's me. Sam Miller."

If that wasn't an alias, I'd turn in my membership card to the Gumshoe Guild. But I *wasn't* a pawn shop copper, so I let it ride.

"Here to redeem." I pulled the yellow ticket from my pocket and held it out.

"*Cowboy painting*," he read, squinting at the ticket. He looked back up at me, even more suspicious. "You're not the guy who brought it in."

"Correct. But I'm the guy who's here to claim it."

He stared at the ticket and chewed his lip, while his nervous fingers picked at a hole in his sweater sleeve. Decision made, he turned around with a sniff. "Wait here." He disappeared through a doorway behind the counter, and I heard him rummaging around and muttering to himself.

Not a minute later he came out carrying a large, framed canvas, holding it by the stretched wire hanger. The back was to me, so all I could see was that the frame was a dark wood. He laid it face up on the counter.

"There you are. One cowboy painting."

And there he was—William S. "Two Gun" Hart, looking out at me. He was standing, holding the reins of a pony I assumed was Fritz—reddish brown with big white patches and four white legs. Green hills rose under a deep blue sky behind them, and at the crest of the highest hill sat La Loma de los Vientos. It was a bright, handsome portrait, but it had the same wistful feeling that I'd sensed in the man himself. He wore that same faraway expression he'd had when I'd seen him gazing out across the valley from his home—a kind of longing for things that had been and no longer were and would never be again. Hart had called it nobility. Maybe so. Friendship and sentiment aside, I could see why the old guy valued it.

"With interest,' Miller said, shaking me out of my daydream. "That's $20.50 I'm due."

"Not today, pal." I reached out and took hold of the frame.

His eyes narrowed, and he took half a step back. "Say, what is this, some kinda stick-up? Who the hell are you, anyway?"

I showed him my license, and he sneered. "A private badge, huh? You ain't got no authority to come in here and—"

CHAPTER SIXTEEN

I held up a hand. "You're absolutely right, bub. But here's the thing—I know, and you know, that this is stolen property. You knew it when it came in. Otherwise, you'd have coughed up more than a double sawbuck. Hell, the frame alone is worth five times that—look at that carving. And the painting? Don't tell me you didn't notice the signature."

He stepped forward again and craned his neck. "C.M. Russell." He looked at me and spread his hands. "So what? I don't know C.M. Russell from Lillian Russell. It's nothing but a picture of a cowboy and a horse to me."

"Okay, let's say just for laughs that that's true." I took out a folded newspaper clipping and spread it on the counter in front of him. It was the *Herald's* account of the Rust/Jones shooting, complete with a photo of Jones—the same one I'd gotten from Aggie.

"This is the guy who brought the painting in, right?"

He looked at the clipping, then at me. His answer was wary, hesitant, more question than answer. "Yeah."

"Well, I'm guessing it won't surprise you to know that he's the lad who pinched it." I tapped the headline with a finger. "Maybe you didn't see it in the news, but he's dead. Thanks to his partner in crime. And that bird's still running around out there somewhere, and he's already killed one other guy and shot a couple more trying to get his hands on this baby." I rattled the frame. "So, do you want to hold on to the painting and wait for him to show up here next, or do you want to be a right guy and help me get it back to its legit owner?"

He looked from the clipping to the painting to me and back again. I could tell he was trying to decide whether he believed me. To help him along, I threw in a kicker. "If you aren't sure, I can call my pals with the burglary/pawn shop detail. They'll be happy to come over and provide you with protection. Of course, they'll crawl up your ass with a magnifying glass while they're here, so your books better be in order."

"All right, all right," he whined. "But have a heart, brother, I'm out twenty bucks on this deal."

I gave him a wink as I picked up the painting. "Cheaper than a funeral."

***

"So, there it is," Walt said when I set the painting in the back seat. "That's what's caused all this ruckus." He'd driven me over in Pooter's deluxe yellow Chrysler convertible. It was a showpiece of a car, and I thought as I climbed into the passenger seat that it suited its errand. One beautiful work of art to transport another.

Walt drove us from there to the Buscadero so he could return the car and I could retrieve my dog. Pooter kindly offered to drive us both from there to my office, but not wanting to inflict Monte's claws on the convertible's butter-soft leather seats, I thanked him anyway and told him we'd take the streetcar.

Pooter and the handful of cowboys in the bar were in awe when I carried the painting in. They gathered around and gaped at it, and remarked on it in hushed tones like they were pilgrims viewing a holy relic.

After they'd all had a gander, I took it with me back to the office so I could use the telephone to ring up Bill Hart. Monte was sleeping on a horse blanket next to the door when I went in. He got up to give the painting a curious sniff as I propped it against the desk. "Watch the nose prints, buddy. This thing is worth more than you, me, and this bar put together."

I sat on the corner of the desk and scratched the dog's big melon head while I dialed Hart's number. The old boy was over the moon to hear that I had his painting in hand, safe and sound. He apologized over and over for all the trouble I'd run into getting it back for him. He felt as guilty about Dusty's getting shot, he said, as if he'd pulled the trigger himself. Probably just one of his dramatic flourishes, I figured, but I tried to convince him he was being too tough on himself. He asked my advice on how he might go about making amends, and I told him that was a topic he'd have to take up with Dusty.

I made arrangements to drive out to his place the next morning and deliver the painting. He brought up my fee, and I told him that conversation would keep until I saw him.

Pooter came in just as I finished the phone call. Before he shut the door, I caught the sound of the cowboys outside firing questions at Walt about

CHAPTER SIXTEEN

Dowd and the shooting in the alley.

Pooter stood looking down at the portrait of Hart. "Sure is a dandy likeness, ain't it?" I said I agreed. He went over to a supply closet and came back with his framed Russell print. "The police got this'n back to me after they took all the fingerprints they needed. I played hell gettin' all that dang black powder scrubbed off.

"You going to hang it back up?"

"I don't reckon. It don't mean to me what it once did. Guess maybe I'll see if one of the boys wants it." He set it down next to the painting and studied them side by side. "That Charlie Russell sure was a painter, though, wasn't he?"

I agreed with that, too. I asked him if I could borrow the Chrysler for my run out to Hart's in the morning. "Walt's usin' it tomorrow," he said. "But I expect he'd be happy to drive you out that way. It'll give him a chance to meet ol' Bill." He looked at the painting again. "What are you doin' with it in the meantime?"

"Keeping it in my office, I guess."

"You ain't worried Chipman might come lookin' for it? Word's bound to get around that you've got it now."

"The office has better locks than my house," I said. "And I can sleep there tonight." I ruffled Monte's ears. "Between me and Call of the Wild here, I think it'll be safe enough."

"Sounds like." Pooter chuckled. "You're bound to get some strange looks, though, carryin' that picture on a streetcar." He gestured to a counter along the wall where they kept a large roll of brown parcel paper for wrapping off-sale bottles. "Maybe you'll want to disguise it first."

I thought that over, and then I stood up and clapped him on the shoulder. "Pooter, did anyone ever tell you that you're a genius?"

Chapter Seventeen

It hadn't been that long, but I felt as though I hadn't been to the office for weeks. I was looking forward to a little quiet time to sit and relax and to handle a few odds and ends. I was also looking forward to a good night's sleep, even if it was in my desk chair.

I leaned the Russell against the wall next to the desk and set the bagged steak sandwich Benjy had fixed me up with down on the blotter. I picked up a few pieces of mail that had been pushed through the slot and dropped them into the tray on my desk on top of the rest of the unopened mail.

I unwrapped the sandwich and was about to dig in when I noticed the envelope on top of the mail stack was addressed to Dr. VanHolton, the dentist in the next office over. I left the sandwich on the desk and, good neighbor that I am, I carried the misdirected mail piece next door to slip it under VanHolton's door, which had no slot. I wasn't gone sixty seconds. When I came back, there was nothing but an empty yellow wrapper on my desk, and Monte was lying on his blanket, gazing up at me with big, innocent eyes. The act was a tough sell, what with the barbecue sauce smeared around his muzzle and in a blotch on his blanket.

"You're supposed to be on the side of law and order, you pirate." He looked at me without a trace of guilt or embarrassment and swiped a paw at the smudge around his wide mouth. "Did you even chew it? Come on."

I took him into the little corner washroom and cleaned up his face. I rinsed out the spot on his blanket in the sink and spread it out on the floor to dry. Monte gave the blanket, then me, an unhappy look. "Blame yourself, pal, not me."

CHAPTER SEVENTEEN

He flopped down on the blanket with a huff, so I left the door open and went back to my desk. I figured I could spend a half hour getting caught up, then go down to Gus's, sans my larcenous hound, and get something else to eat.

I turned on the radio, tuned into Jack Benny on KFI, and sat down again. After sorting through all the accumulated mail, I spent a few minutes writing out checks to pay a few bills. If it hadn't been for the radio, I might have heard the footsteps.

The bell dingus on my door jingled, and I looked up just as the elusive Chipman himself stepped into the room. I stood halfway up out of reflex, but the big automatic held low in his right hand checked me. My .380 was lying next to the mail tray, where I'd put it when I sat down. Chipman noticed my eyes flicking to my own gun and smiled.

"You'll never reach it in time. But you're welcome to give it a try." His left arm was in a sling, and he raised it a bit. "I owe you at least one bullet for this."

"What do you want, Duane?" I didn't need to ask. I just wanted to keep him talking.

His eyes went blank at the question; then he smiled even wider. "So, you puzzled it out, did you? I guess you think you're a pretty smart fellow."

"My mother always said so."

He smirked. "If your mama was right, then you should know what I want. The first thing is there yonder." He pointed his chin toward the parcel, leaning against the wall.

"Yeah, you've gone to a whole lot of trouble to get your hands on it, haven't you?"

"Had to. The fellow who wanted it wanted it so bad he paid me half up front. I won't tell you how much—I'm not the braggin' type. But I will say it was a whole lot more than the five thousand Ty Jones was gonna settle for, the dumb peckerwood."

"And I'm guessing this isn't the kind of buyer who would be too understanding if you couldn't deliver what he'd already paid you half for."

"You could put it that way." He motioned toward the painting with his gun's muzzle. "Out of curiosity, where'd Ty have it hid?"

"Pawnshop. Not a bad idea, really. It was safe enough there, and he could get it back whenever he needed it, so long as he held on to the ticket."

He blew out a breath, shook his head. "That sneaky son of a bitch. Served him right to get himself shot dead."

"What about Leo Rust? What did you have against him?"

"Nothin' in particular. I was just lookin' to get a line on the painting, but he decided to try and get tough with me."

"Yeah, but I'm talking about setting him up for a murder charge with Jones."

He shrugged. "What can I say? Opportunity knocked. I wanted Ty gone, and I knew with the bad blood between 'em Rust couldn't resist shootin' at him, even if it was only a blank. I just made sure it wasn't."

"Cute. So, what's the other thing?"

"Other thing?"

"You said the Russell was the first thing you wanted. So what's left?"

The smirk vanished. "Maybe you ain't so smart at that." He kept the gun on me as he sidled over to the radio. He shifted the auto to the hand poking out of the sling. "Don't fool yourself that I can't still pull the trigger on you," he said as his right hand started fiddling with the radio dial.

"Not a Benny fan, I guess?"

"I'm just lookin' for something more..." He searched for the word. "... appropriate." He turned the dial through quick snatches of swing, jazz, a hellfire sermon... I thought he might stop when I heard Gene Autry, but he moved on past until the sound of police sirens, squealing tires, and tommy guns blared out.

He smiled again. "*Gangbusters*. That'll do just fine." He moved the pistol to his right hand again. "See, the other thing I want is to get you off my back trail, permanent-like. I'm tired of duckin' your shadow." He raised the gun.

The racket on the radio faded to the background as a somber voice came on over it, describing how the police were closing the net around the Rubberhead Gordon mob at last. Over the droning narrator another sound rose—a deep, threatening, animal growl, not coming from the radio, but from just behind Chipman.

CHAPTER SEVENTEEN

He darted a quick glance over his shoulder, long enough to spot Monte standing in the washroom doorway. He was in a half crouch, the fur on his muscular shoulders bristling. His eyes were narrow and angry, and his lips were peeled back to show off his impressive fangs right up to the gum line. Strings of saliva hung from his jaws. Mixed with the leftover barbecue sauce in his mouth, it looked like dripping blood. A nice touch, I thought.

"You're in a pickle now, Duane," I said. "You can pull the trigger, but you won't get off more than one shot before he's got those teeth buried in your jugular. I've seen it before. It's not pretty."

"So maybe I just shoot him first." His voice was losing some of its confident edge.

"You could do that, I guess. But I can guarantee you'll need more than one round. And you'll have to turn around to do it, because if you miss, well..."

All the cockiness faded from his face, along with most of the color. His eyes wobbled, uncertain. I could see he was figuring his odds, and not liking them.

"And as soon as you turn around," I went on, "I'm going to go for my gun, and I'm not likely to miss. And I promise you that if you hurt my dog, before I put your miserable, murdering ass down for good, I'll put the first two bullets in your balls."

He tensed as I reached over to take hold of the top of the paper-wrapped frame. I brought it around and set it down again, leaning it against the front of the desk.

"Look, pal, I think there's been enough blood shed over this damn thing. Nobody needs to get shot here tonight. Take it and go on your merry way—I won't stop you. Maybe we'll meet again sometime, and then we can pick up where we left off. Or maybe after you collect your other half for it, you'll have enough jack to disappear for good. I'm willing to roll the dice if you are."

He eyed me with suspicion but transferred his gun to his left hand again. His eyes darted right, trying to see Monte without turning his head.

"That mutt ain't gonna jump me if I move, is he?"

"Not as long as you go slow and keep your gat quiet." He hesitated, then slowly reached out and shut the radio off. When he took a tentative half step forward, Monte turned his volume up a notch.

"Easy, boy." Chipman seemed unsure whether I meant that for him or the dog. He stopped dead. Monte read my tone and took his growling down to a purr. Bit by bit Chipman slid his foot forward another half step, like he was walking on ice.

One more halting step and he had his hand on the frame. He kept his eyes steady on me, but I could see him straining to catch Monte in his side vision. He dragged the frame toward him and lifted it clear of the floor, then started backing away with the same shuffling steps. The strain was showing—lines of sweat ran down his face and he blinked his eyes to keep them clear of it. He stopped moving when he felt the door at his back.

He had both me and Monte in his field of view then, and I could tell he was weighing the odds again. He must've reached the same conclusion as before, because he set the frame down against the wall and reached back for the doorknob. He eased the door open, watching me the whole time. He backed out into the hallway and dragged the parcel around to lean it against the outer wall. He stood framed in the open doorway and gave me a long, searching look. Then a fresh smirk wiped the strain from his face.

"Congratulations, Duane," I said. "You win. This round."

He winked as though it was never in doubt and reached out to pull the door shut. I heard him pick up his prize and start quick-stepping down the back stairs. The alley door opened and closed, and he was gone.

Chapter Eighteen

"I wish your pop could have come along," I told Walt as he navigated the big car up the hill. "He was here at the start of this loony case—hell, he *did* start it. It would be nice for him to be here for the finish."

"He'd like that all right. But the doctors want to hold him for another few days at least. He wouldn't want you to put this off for his sake." He tipped his head toward the painting lying on the back seat. "It's high time it went back home."

"You're right. It's been gone long enough."

He gave me a quick look. "I'm curious. How do you know Chipman won't come back when he figures out you've duped him?"

"I don't, for sure," I said. "But the hurry he seemed to be in, I'm betting he was going to take that package straight to his buyer."

Walt laughed. "I'd like to have seen the look on their faces when they found out all they had was Pooter's old print."

"You and me both, pal."

"How do you suppose that scene went?"

"Not well."

"Where did you keep this one in the meantime?"

"Left it at the bar with Pooter. Stashed in his supply closet. I didn't figure Chipman would go looking there again. And if he did, he'd have run into Pooter and Joe Lopez camping out with a couple of shotguns."

I could sense Walt's excitement as we wound our way up past the monument to Fritz, the bunkhouse, the guard tower. He'd told me that as a kid he and his granddad had gone to the local movie house nearly every week, and Hart's

Westerns were particular favorites for the two of them. His grandfather—Dusty's father—had driven cattle up the Chisholm Trail as a youngster, and Walt said the films always seemed to bring those days to life again for the old man. For days afterward he'd tell stories of the wild adventures he'd had, and the colorful sights he'd seen and characters he'd met. For his part, Walt said, he always liked that Hart's movies tended to be morality tales instead of the standard, humdrum, Hollywood shoot-'em-ups.

"Good Lord," he said as we crested the hill, and he caught sight of the big Spanish Colonial house.

I couldn't help but smile. "You haven't seen anything yet. Wait'll we go inside."

He slowed the car to a crawl as we got closer so he could take in the whole picture—the house, the grounds, the view of the city so distant and far below. When we reached the house, he stopped, set the brake, and stepped out of the car in one smooth motion. He turned in a slow circle with his mouth half open and a look of wonder in his eyes. I've never been there myself, but I was guessing the Texas plains didn't have scenery to compete with this.

Walt was so engrossed in his gawping he didn't even notice the stately old guy in the cowboy sombrero approaching from the house. He turned with a startled jerk when Hart spoke.

"Welcome, gentlemen!" he called out in his stagy voice.

The scenery had plenty dazzled Walt, but it didn't half prepare him for the jolt of seeing his boyhood hero standing a dozen feet away, life-sized and in full color. I'd never known a lawyer to be speechless before—wouldn't have even believed it was possible—but Walt seemed to have completely forgotten how his tongue operated. When I introduced them and Hart shook his hand, all Walt could do was make a sort of mumbling noise that sounded vaguely like "Pleasure."

Hart responded to the marble-mouthed greeting with a gracious smile. I supposed he was used to encountering star-struck fans. He welcomed me like we were old pals, and his eyes lit up like Klieg lights when I lifted the brown-wrapped parcel from the backseat.

He ushered us inside, and we followed him upstairs to the big living room.

CHAPTER EIGHTEEN

Walt's eyes were like pinwheels as he took in all the sights along the way. I was behind him going up the spiral staircase, and I kept a tight grip on the twisting balustrade the whole time. Walt was so distracted looking all around him I worried that he'd miss his footing and tumble us both back down the stairs.

We made it to the top safely and Walt continued to goggle at all the art pieces along the hallway. I heard a sharp intake of breath when we crossed the threshold into the living room, as he took in the beams, the artwork, the colorful rugs and other furnishings.

Hart's own eyes hardly left the package I carried, but he was too courtly a gent to rush things. He installed Walt and me on the sofa while he went over to a serving cart that held a silver coffee urn and insisted on first pouring us each a cup. Coffee in hand, he took his seat next to the fireplace and looked closely at Walt.

"I believe I'd have known you even without the introduction, Mr. VanNeer. You strongly favor your father."

"Walt, please." He seemed to have found his voice somehow.

Hart put him even more at ease with a couple minutes of small talk—Walt's job, his home, his impressions of Los Angeles, that sort of stuff. Meanwhile, I just sat and sipped my coffee.

The niceties observed, Hart came around at last to the business at hand. He turned his attention to me. "I suppose I should open this gift you've brought me, eh, Nate?"

I handed the painting across to him. He laid it on his lap and took out a small pocket knife to cut the twine. He pulled off the wrapping, dropped it on the floor, and let out a gasp as he sat looking at his own likeness on the canvas. With a bony hand on either side of the big frame, he lifted the painting upright to better catch the light. Tears spilled down his furrowed cheeks, and his moist eyes got that same dreamy, far-off look I'd come to recognize. He started to say something, but the words seemed to clog his gullet. He swallowed hard, then loudly cleared his throat. When he managed to get words out at last, his voice had none of that affected, dramatic tone that was his habit. He was just a plain-spoken guy saying what was on his mind.

"I can't tell you how grateful I am to you for this, Nate. And Walt—I know you had a hand in this, too." He knuckled away the tears. "You've made me one happy old hombre."

He carried the painting over and hung it in its place on the wall. He stood back and stared at it for a long time. As I watched him, I had the strange feeling that even though I could clearly see him standing there, he wasn't in the room with us any longer. He'd gone somewhere else, someplace far away in time. Wherever it was, I suspected his old pal Fritz was there with him. When he came back, he'd lost the misty look, and he turned brisk and businesslike.

"Now," he said, going to the secretary and opening the drawer, "It's time we settle affairs." He took out a familiar thick, brown envelope, and before I could protest, he walked over and tossed it into my lap. "You've more than earned that, I dare say."

I looked in the envelope. I didn't count it but was certain it was the five grand ransom money.

"Bill, listen—"

He sat again and held out a hand to stop me. "This is a business matter, and I'm a fair-dealing man. If this is insufficient, feel free to say so."

"It's more than sufficient, that's the thing."

We spent the next ten minutes haggling over my payment for the job. I insisted he was overpaying while he was adamant he wasn't paying anywhere near enough. We batted it back and forth without making any headway until Walt, being a lawyer and probably not able to help himself, waded in to play arbitrator. With a savvy that would have done Solomon proud, he steered us to what I thought was a pretty good compromise. I'd accept five hundred dollars, which would go to fixing the damage to my car and to Arnie's pickup with a little left over, and Hart would take care of Dusty's medical bills. The second part was a tough sell, only because Hart insisted he'd been planning to do that anyway. But in the end, Walt got him to agree to terms.

With the financial arrangements out of the way, Hart became the gallant host again. He gave Walt an even lengthier tour of the house and grounds

CHAPTER EIGHTEEN

than I'd had with Dusty. Since I'd had the tour already, I left them to it while I went out on the balcony and enjoyed another cup of coffee, the fresh air, and the spectacular view. The big city looked different from there—smaller, more peaceful, almost inviting. Maybe that was the trick—maybe L.A. was only meant to be viewed from a distance.

Chapter Nineteen

It looked like a scene from a western movie—not a Poverty Row cheapie with a bare-bones cast and a budget smaller than a PTA coffee fund, but one of the big, cast-heavy pictures they made at RKO or Universal. The kind that hired the Gower Gulch boys and girls by the busload.

But from the looks of things the studios, big and small, must have taken a day off because the busloads were all in this one spot. The sprawling green lawn of La Loma de los Vientos was a sea of cowboy hats. Every Western day player in Hollywood, plus more than a few well-known actors, had turned out at Hart's invitation to welcome Dusty Vanner back to the land of the living. Hart hadn't gone on the cheap, either. He had three honest-to-goodness chuck wagons set up next to freshly dug campfire pits and serving up slabs of barbecued beef, fried potatoes, beans, corn on the cob, and sourdough biscuits. The meal was capped off with peach cobbler cooked in big Dutch ovens and smothered under softball-sized scoops of hand-cranked ice cream. A long bar set up near the chuckwagons dispensed cold bottles of beer and warm shots of whiskey, and the crowd seemed to be keeping the bartenders twice as busy as the cooks.

The picnic tables under the big-top sized canopy on the broad lawn only held about half of the assembly. The remainder of the crowd sat in clusters on blankets spread on the grass or just milled around eating, drinking, and chattering.

A stage was set up at one end of the wide green with the far-off landscape of the city at the performers' backs. Hart had lined up a whole slate of entertainment—there were fiddlers, a western swing band, a couple of

CHAPTER NINETEEN

yodeling cowboy singers, a guy doing fancy rope tricks and gun spinning.

The doctors had booted Dusty the day before on the condition that he take it easy for a while. Walt had promised to sheepdog him and make sure he didn't overdo it. I didn't envy the guy that job. I sat at a table under the canvas with him, Walt, and Pooter. From my vantage point, I could keep an eye on Monte, who was frolicking at the opposite end of the wide green with his new best friend, Gal.

We'd saved a spot for our host, but he'd been in motion without letup since the party started, greeting each new arrival, seeing to the guests already there, checking on the food and drink, and announcing the entertainers. I was amazed that a guy his age had so much energy.

Once it seemed like everyone who was coming had arrived and everything was running smoothly, Hart finally joined us at the table.

"This is quite the shindig you put on, Bill," Dusty said. "I appreciate it, but you didn't have to go to all this trouble."

"Nonsense, old friend. It was the very least I could do."

"Now *that there's* nonsense," Dusty answered. "You've done plenty enough already."

We all knew what he was talking about. He'd kicked and fussed when he found out that Hart was planning to foot his hospital and doctor bills. Hart had stood firm, and Walt had stepped in to negotiate another compromise. Hart could pay the bills, but he could never pay for another drink at the Buscadero if he lived to be a thousand.

We'd all pretty much eaten and drunk our fill at that point, but Hart insisted on a toast. Walt whispered something to him, and he got up to speak to one of the bartenders, then took his seat again. The guy came over a minute later carrying a tray of drinks and handed out four whiskeys. Dusty made a disgusted sound when the bartender set a club soda in front of him—he was teetotaling on doctor's orders. He shot Walt an accusing look and Walt turned his palms up in a "don't blame me" gesture.

Hart lifted his glass, and we all followed suit. "To my old compadre, Dusty Vanner. May he be riding the open range again as soon as may be."

We all clinked glasses and drank. Dusty made an exaggerated face as he took a gulp of the soda. He saluted Hart with the glass. "Bill, I thank you for the spirit, if not the spirits."

Hart gave a gracious nod, then stood and laid a hand on Dusty's shoulder. "If you'll excuse me, gents, I have one more ceremonial duty to perform."

He walked toward the stage and, seeing him coming, the bird sawing a fiddle up there finished his tune and bowed his thanks for the applause. Hart took the stage, and the crowd started to quiet down. He looked out over the gathered company until every voice was hushed, then addressed us in his stage orator's voice.

"Ladies and gentlemen, buckaroos and buckarettes. I thank you deeply for your presence here and for your kind indulgence as I tender a few remarks. As you know, I'm a man of few words—"

"Since when?" yelled an inebriated voice from the crowd.

Hart paused with a patient smile. When the smattering of laughter faded away, he continued. "And I am, after all, but a humble thespian."

"Since when?" called another voice, and this time the crowd roared.

Hart was unfazed. He stood smiling until the hullabaloo died down again. "But today we are here to pay tribute to an authentic man of the West..."

"Aw, shit," Dusty muttered. He cast his eyes around, looking for an escape route. Walt laid a hand on his arm and shook his head, and Dusty dropped his shoulders with a defeated sigh.

"...against whose glories of yore," Hart went on, "Hollywood's most thrilling epics pale in comparison. A man whose courage and fortitude are only exceeded by his steadfast loyalty to kith and kin alike, and who now, in the autumn of his life's bold saga..."

He went on at this rate for another five minutes. All the while, Dusty looked more and more miserable. He hunkered down in his seat, trying to make himself invisible. He looked over at me as Hart was winding down.

"Never thought I'd miss that hospital bed," he said with a pained grin.

On stage, Hart took his hat off and held it over his heart. "Our *querido amigo*, Dusty Vanner." He bowed so deeply I thought he'd crack his head on the stage.

The crowd broke loose with so much hand clapping, foot stomping, and

CHAPTER NINETEEN

cheering, people in the city must have been upping their earthquake insurance. Not knowing what else to do, Dusty half stood and gave the whooping throng a grim smile and an embarrassed little wave. He looked ill as a voice in the pack, then another, then several more, cried out, "Speech! Speech!"

He looked at his son and his companions for rescue. Without missing a beat, we each took up the cry, "Speech! Speech!"

The helpless look he gave us turned to black murder. He stood and made his way forward, and the cheers and applause only increased the closer he got to the stage. Before he mounted the platform, he shot one last look at us over his shoulder, shaking his head at our treason.

Once he was on the stage, the hubbub faded, and it got as quiet as things could ever be with a couple hundred half-drunk cowboys in the mix. Dusty stood and looked out over the mass of well-wishers for a long while, like he was trying to memorize each and every face. He lifted his hat off, and when he opened his mouth to speak, even the tipsy laughter and chatter died away.

"Aw, hell," he said, turning his hat in both hands. "Thanks." With a wave of the hat, he stepped down to even more clamor than before and slowly made his way back to his seat. Walt and Pooter both clapped him on the back as he sat down.

I leaned in to catch his eye. "That was quite a speech, Mussolini."

He hit me with a blank stare. "Do you ever wonder why it is you ain't got any other friends but me?"

"It keeps me up nights." I gave him a light punch in the shoulder. "Good to have you back, old man."

Chapter Twenty

"So, Dusty tells me you're staying on out here once he's all back to normal," I said. "Whatever the hell *that* is."

"I am," Walt said. "I kind of like it out here in the big city."

We were sitting at the bar in the Buscadero, enjoying some welcome peace and quiet after the boisterous barbecue at Hart's ranch the day before. It was early, and so far we had the place to ourselves. Pooter, who almost never drank while he was behind the bar, had broken his personal protocol to join us in a cold beer.

"I'm taking the bar exam next month," Walt said, draining the last of his beer, "Until then, I guess I'm just on vacation."

Pooter snatched the empty mug from Walt's hand before it touched the bar. "Some vacation," he said with a snort as he refilled the mug. "Lookin' after that ornery old cuss." He slid the fresh beer in front of Walt. "There you go. A little more hair of the dog."

I looked at my watch. "Speaking of dogs, how far were they going to walk?"

"Just twice around the block." Walt turned and glanced out through the half-glass doors. "Pa's supposed to go slow for a couple of weeks."

Dusty was restless after his extended bed stay, and the doctors had told him a little walking wouldn't hurt him as long as he didn't overdo it. So, he was out giving Monte his daily exercise.

Not two minutes later, the two of them came in. Monte was bright-eyed and peppy, and Dusty was a little winded.

"Sit yourself, pard," Pooter told him. "I'll get you a drink. What'll you have?"

Dusty took a seat and pointed at the mug in Walt's hand.

CHAPTER TWENTY

Pooter cocked his head. "I *meant*, do you want ginger ale or club soda?" He turned to get a glass. "I guess you get club soda."

"*Blah.*" Dusty backhanded the air, doing his best imitation of Queenan. "Some friend you are." He leaned down to unhook Monte's leash, and the big brute mounted the stool next to me, paws on the bar.

Pooter set a bowl of water between Monte's paws and the mutt splashed his tongue around in it. Then Pooter plunked a glass of club soda down for Dusty.

"Why does the dog get his drink before I do?"

"'Cause I like him better, that's why. He's not a cantankerous old bastard."

"I'll have you know my parents were married." Dusty took a disgusted sip of his drink. He was still muttering and sulking over it a few minutes later when the door opened again, and Bill Hart walked in.

"Good day, gentlemen!" He shook hands with us each in turn, with as much enthusiasm as if he hadn't seen us in months. "I'm pleased to find you all here. I trust you enjoyed yourselves at our little fiesta yesterday."

We all assured him we had. He told us he had a few errands to run in the city and wanted to stop by to make sure that the festivities hadn't taxed Dusty too much. Dusty answered that he was feeling fine, if a little tired, but added—with a dark look at Pooter—that was nothing a beer or two wouldn't mend.

Bill took the stool next to Dusty and politely declined Pooter's offer of a drink. He made casual chitchat with us for ten minutes or so and made quite a fuss over Monte, who—always able to spot a dog lover—had taken an instant liking to the old actor.

I had the impression the entire time that Hart had something more on his mind. Once the small talk ran out, he got around to it.

"It's been a pleasure, boys," he said as he dismounted his stool and gave Monte's chin a final scratch. "I must be getting back to the hacienda, but first, I have something in the car I'd like to leave with you if you'll allow me a moment."

He went out and came back shortly carrying what I mistook at first for Pooter's old Russell print, although the frame was wider and fancier. It was exactly the same scene—pistol-waving cowboys riding their horses through the doors of a hotel—but when he laid it on the bar, I could see the brush strokes on the canvas surface.

"Pooter," Hart began, "Nate explained to me how you sacrificed your signed print to help return my portrait to me, and I want to give this to you in recompense." He turned to Dusty. "And to you, my old friend, as a sign of my gratitude."

Dusty was speechless—a rare thing—and Pooter was about to protest when Hart went on. "I'm embarrassed to say it's been wasted merely hanging in the bunkhouse at the ranch." He looked at the empty spot on the wall behind the bar. "I think it might find a much more appreciative audience here." He gestured to the blank space. "May I?"

Pooter looked at Dusty, and Dusty nodded.

"You may, Bill," he said.

Hart slipped behind the bar and hung the piece. He fiddled a moment to get it level, then took a half step back to admire the effect. His eye fell on the framed photo of his younger self, and a melancholy smile flashed across his face.

He stepped out from behind the bar, walked straight to the doors, then stopped and turned. He drew himself up to his full height and filled his lungs. When he spoke, he might have been addressing a packed theater instead of an audience of four plus a dog.

"Gentlemen, I thank you sincerely for your many kindnesses, and I bid you good day. Please know that the doors of La Loma de los Vientos will ever be open to you. *Adios, mis mejores amigos.*" He snatched his hat off, made a wide, sweeping gesture with it, and followed it out the door.

Chapter Twenty-One

Three days after Hart's barbecue, Monte and I took a walk in the park after lunch and had just gotten back to the office. Monte was napping, and I was giving the place a long overdue dusting when the phone rang.

"Nate Ross."

"Ross—Queenan here." As though there was ever any doubt.

"What can I do for you, Cap?"

"Me? Nothing. This is me doing something for you. As usual."

"Okay, I'll bite. What can *you* do for *me*?"

"Well, I just had some news come across my desk I thought might interest you. Got a call yesterday from the sheriff's department in San Bernardino County. I guess some old prospector, rock hound, or what have you, was puttering around in the desert out around Daggett—wherever the hell that is—a couple of days ago, and he found a body. Well, what the coyotes left of one. Couple of bullets in it—one in the chest, one in the head. Had a Republic Pictures check stub in the pocket made out to Pete Chipman."

"No kidding." I'd suspected I might get a call like this one day. I just didn't think it would be so soon. It looked like Chipman's buyer couldn't take a joke.

"Anyway," Queenan went on, "They wired us the prints, and we checked them against Chipman's—Duane, that is, not Pete. It's him all right. No doubts. So, I guess you and me can quit lookin' now."

"I guess we can."

His voice took on a suspicious edge. "You don't sound all that surprised.

You don't know somethin' I should know, do you?"

"All I know is it sounds like he's San Berdoo's problem now."

The pause on the line lasted so long, I thought maybe we'd lost our connection. I was about to jiggle the switch hook when I heard Queenan's low chuckle.

"Yeah, I guess you're right, at that. All the cases this clears for us, who am I to look a gift horse in the mouth? There's just one more thing."

"What's that?"

"Well, bein' as how this means I found Chipman before you did, I'll be expectin' that bottle of Scotch. And not the cheap stuff, either."

"You know what, Cap? Let's make it *two* bottles."

"Two? What are you talkin'..." He sighed. "You know what? I don't even want to know. I guess I'll see you around, Ross."

"Not if I see you first."

* * *

After talking to Queenan, we had a quiet afternoon in the office. Monte caught up on his napping, and I finally got all the bills up to date and checks ready to go out in the afternoon mail. Nobody came in with a knotty problem they wanted me to untangle, and no hard guys showed up to threaten me with guns.

I poured myself a generous bourbon, set fire to a cigar, and leaned back with my feet on the desk, ready to celebrate the lull. I'd just closed my eyes to better savor the sweet sound of nothing but Monte's gentle snoring when I heard soft footsteps in the hall. The bell over my door jangled me out of my trance and caused Monte to wake up with a snort.

A freckle-faced messenger boy sidled in, a pair of tinted motorcycle goggles pushed up above the bill of his uniform cap. He swept a curious eye around the room. Maybe he'd never been in a real live gumshoe's office before. It didn't seem to impress him much.

"Parcel for Nate Ross," he said in a businesslike way. He looked from me to the yawning dog and back again, like he was unsure which of us he should

CHAPTER TWENTY-ONE

be addressing.

I dropped my shoes to the floor and tapped my cigar on the brass nameplate on the desk. "That'd be me." He handed me a flat package a couple of inches thick and about a foot square. I signed his book, and he flicked his cap brim with a finger and left without another word.

Nothing on the kraft paper wrapping gave me a clue as to who had sent the parcel. I tore the paper off, and inside was a glass-fronted frame of blond wood. Behind the glass, it held a pen and ink sketch on heavy, cream-colored paper. The first thing that caught my eye was a now-familiar signature in the bottom right—"C.M. Russell"—above a small buffalo skull.

The sketch itself was an outdoor scene, a hilly meadow with mountains in the far background. A stern-looking man on a tall horse was holding a Winchester rifle leveled on two guys—outlaws, from the look of them—who were on the ground. One knelt with his hands up, and the other was just crawling out of his bedroll, rubbing sleep out of his eyes. The fellow with the rifle wore a rain slicker over his coat, and with his free hand, he was pulling them both aside to show the boys the star pinned on his chest.

I turned the frame over and read an inscription written on the backing. It said:

To Nate Ross, un buen buscador y amigo.
Very sincerely,
Bill Hart.

"I'll be damned." I went over to my bookshelves and pulled out a dog-eared Spanish-English dictionary left over from my short-lived college days. *Amigo*, I understood well enough. *Buscador* was a mystery to me, although I was pretty sure it didn't mean saloon keeper. According to the dictionary it meant "seeker, searcher, or hunter." I thought about that for a while. The more I thought, the more I liked the sound of it. Maybe I'd change the lettering on my office door to "Nate Ross, Buscador." It might give the place a little more pizzazz.

* * *

When we got home, and I'd fed Monte and had a sandwich myself, I hung the Russell sketch over the small fireplace in the living room. I sat back in my chair, a drink in my hand and Monte lounging at my feet, and stared at the picture for a long time.

Afterward I opened up the newspaper, curious to see what had become of the city and the world while I'd been busy chasing paintings and cowboys and killers. I was in too good a mood to start reading the front-page stuff about the situation in Europe, so I went straight to the second section. At the bottom of the third page, below all the celebrity gossip, I noticed a large ad for a double feature at a drive-in theater in Burbank. I wasn't a moviegoer as a rule, but one of the films, the ad said, was a re-release of *Tumbleweeds*, William S. Hart's last movie. The title seemed familiar. I thought about it for a bit and dragged up a vague memory of going to see it with my old man not long after I graduated high school.

I looked at Monte. "You ever been to a drive-in movie, pal?" He grinned up at me and winked his eyes. "Yeah, me neither." Thinking more about it, I figured it was the least I could do for the old man—watch him head off into the sunset for the very last time.

I put the paper aside, grabbed my coat and hat, and snapped my fingers at Monte.

"Come on, you old buscador, you. Let's ride."

About the Author

J.R. Sanders is a native Midwesterner and longtime denizen of the L.A. suburbs. A former police officer and private investigator, J.R.'s nonfiction articles appear in such magazines as Law & Order and Wild West. His nonfiction books cover topics as diverse as Southern California apple farms and Old West lawmen killed in the line of duty. His first Nate Ross novel, *Stardust Trail*, was a 2021 Spur Award Finalist (for Best Historical Novel), and Silver Falchion Award Finalist (for Best Investigator). *Dead-Bang Fall*, the second Nate Ross novel, was a 2023 Shamus Award winner for Best Paperback P.I. Novel.

J.R. lives in Southern California with his wife, Rose, and their rescue dogs, Ruby and Marlowe.

SOCIAL MEDIA HANDLES:
   Facebook: facebook.com/jrsanderswest
   Instagram: instagram.com/jrsanderswest
   LinkTree: linktr.ee/jrsanders
   https://jrsanders.com/contact

AUTHOR WEBSITE:

www.jrsanders.com

Also by J.R. Sanders

Bring the Night (Level Best Books, 2023)

Dead-Bang Fall (Level Best Books, 2022)

Stardust Trail (Level Best Books, 2020)

Some Gave All: Forgotten Old West Lawmen Who Died With Their Boots On (Moonlight Mesa Associates, 2013)

www.ingramcontent.com/pod-product-compliance
Lightning Source LLC
Chambersburg PA
CBHW031719281224
19486CB00001B/58